LOVE
SEX
TRAVEL
MUSIK

LOVE
SEX
TRAVEL
MUSIK

RODGE GLASS

**FREIGHT
BOOKS**

First published April 2013

Freight Books
49-53 Virginia Street
Glasgow, G1 1TS
www.freightbooks.co.uk

A CIP catalogue reference for this book is available from the British Library

ISBN 978-1-908754-16-5
ISBN ebook 978-1-908754-17-2

Typeset by Freight in Plantin
Printed and bound by Bell and Bain, Glasgow

the publisher acknowledges investment from
Creative Scotland toward the publication of this book

CONTENTS

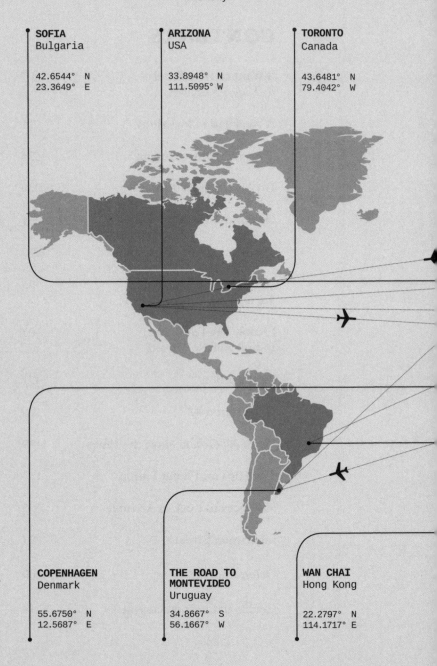

SOFIA
Bulgaria

42.6544° N
23.3649° E

ARIZONA
USA

33.8948° N
111.5095° W

TORONTO
Canada

43.6481° N
79.4042° W

COPENHAGEN
Denmark

55.6750° N
12.5687° E

**THE ROAD TO
MONTEVIDEO**
Uruguay

34.8667° S
56.1667° W

WAN CHAI
Hong Kong

22.2797° N
114.1717° E

The Sky

MANCHESTER
England

53.4800° N
2.2400°   W

ROME
Italy

41.9000° N
12.5000° E

KRAKOW
Poland

50.0614° N
19.9372° E

HAMMAMET
Tunisia

36.4000° N
10.6167° E

A BEACH
North Africa

29.9569° N
15.7461° E

**THE AMAZON
RAINFOREST**
Brazil

3.1600° S
60.0300° W

For Haim

I WANT TO BE A TOURIST

by Kapka Kassabova

I imagine my life as a city
somewhere in the third world, or the second.
And I want to be a tourist
in the city of my life.

I want to stroll in shorts and baseball hat,
with laminated maps and dangling cameras.
I want to find things for the first time.
Look, they were put there just for me!

I want a room with musty curtains.
I want a view of rubbish dumps and urchins.
I want food poisoning, the dust of traffic
in the mouth, the thrill of others' misery.

Let me be a tourist in the city of my life.
Give me overpriced coffee in the square,
let me visit briefly the mausoleum of the past
and photograph its mummy,

give me the open sewers, the stunted dreams,
the jubilation of ruins, the lepers, the dogs,
give me signs in a funny language that I never
have to learn. Then take my money and let me go.

Guztia espero nuen eman duten gozamenerako eta [...] konbentzitu me bidaia izan etsita me ekiteko, baina oso, berriz, ustekabeko hezkuntza bat eskuratu dut.

A WEEKEND
OF FREEDOM

This time last year I was melting. I could hardly persuade myself to get up for work in the mornings. My marriage was no marriage at all. All I'd ever wanted was to be able to afford good suits without having to check the price tag, but recently the fat salary my Dad would have killed for had been somehow getting sucked away from me, going on an overambitious mortgage, on bills, on five different-but-apparently-all-thoroughly-essential types of insurance, on taxes, two cars, a pension: the rest was wasted on expensive wine I didn't appreciate. Meals in restaurants with menus entirely in French.

Heather said I wasn't awake anymore — even my only hobby wasn't really mine. I searched out old war memorabilia, First and Second World War mainly, a habit and a collection inherited from my Dad. *They're my little containers of history,* he said. *Not always beautiful, but then, things of value rarely are.* One piece was a regimental cigarette case with an engraving explaining it had been presented to a soldier by the Princess Mary Christmas Fund in 1914. I kept that one in a special locked glass case. Heather often asked what happened to the man she fell in love with. Well, you don't notice it happening. Life just gets gradually narrower, until a ray of sun is enough to make a good day and a splash of rain is enough to make a bad one.

Then two things happened in the same week: first, I got made redundant. Cutbacks due to *challenging economic circumstances.* In a month's time I'd be jobless. Nothing personal, they said, though my boss's expression when he broke the news suggested otherwise. The second thing was Greenie phoning to say he'd been offered a five year construction contract in Dubai. Well, he couldn't say no. Nobody gets five year contracts these days, do they? God knows what they wanted him for but hey, who was he to argue? *It's wild out there,* he said. *Seriously. Those bastard Sheiks are shitting money.*

Everyone else seemed to be getting offered exotic stints abroad. Even Greenie, the stupid fuck, was jetting off into the sunset, while I was still stuck here in the cold. He explained he was having a lads-only going-away party, abroad. *Where's the destination?* I asked. He replied, *Doesn't matter, does it? Some hole in Eastern Europe. Smith's coming. Finn too. Even Tommy.* They got together all the time. I hadn't seen any of that lot for two years, maybe three, maybe longer. I couldn't think of an excuse so I said, *When do we leave? My November just freed up...* Greenie talked fast. *It'll be great to have everyone together again. Finn's been before so he can show us the best spots. He reckons the birds out there are well hot — no fatties. Not enough food to go round for that. And they'll do anything for a euro!*

I expected Heather to complain about me going away without her, but no. *Go out there and have fun,* she said, flashing a rare smile. *But bring me back something nice. Something little, like you get at those lovely European markets.*

I told her: *I don't know about that, I've heard this place we're going to is a real dive.* I still packed my best shirts though. Finn knew this fetish club that was strictly members only (unless of course you looked loaded), which showed a hardcore live lesbian sex show on tv in the toilets. *You can get off on the action going on in the next room while you're taking a shit,* he told me at the airport before we left, as if that was a perfectly ordinary thing to say. He and Tommy had been planning this thing for a while.

We arrived on the Friday morning. Tommy had booked us all into this cheap hotel (well, cheap for us but too expensive for the locals) with a special suite in a separate building out the back. Not glamorous, but perfect for our needs. We dumped our stuff and hit the bars straight away, the first of many toasts to Greenie's new life coming just before noon. We drank hard all day and only bothered to eat one meal, where we ordered steak, told the waiters to speak English, stood on the chairs between courses and belted out football chants to the tune of the traditional folk music being played by the restaurant guitar player. I felt like I was eighteen again, centre of attention, forgetting myself. Forgetting everything. I sang till I was hoarse, ignored the prices on the tattered menus and bought drinks for the entire place. Lying outside on the road after that meal, the North Star spinning above me, I considered hooking up with a local girl and never going home. Then a car nearly ran me over, we swore at the driver as we escaped, ran away like kids into the next street and I forgot about the idea. Finn ushered us into a nearby club.

I only realised what kind of place it was when I ordered our drinks and noticed the girl dancing nearly naked on a pole attached to the bar, her high heels at my eye level, getting in the way as I tried to hand over the money. I burst out laughing. Right then, everything was funny.

The girl on the bar was laughing at something too. We all clinked glasses, cheered our weekend of freedom and took the piss out of Tommy while he got a lap dance right there in his seat, still holding his beer. Finn and Greenie paid for a dance too, with the same girl, who was maybe eighteen, maybe nineteen, but looked like a pro who was *born* doing it. She was obviously thinking about something else and didn't complain until Finn felt her arse while she was waving it so close to his nose that she was virtually touching him anyway. After we'd been chucked out by the bouncers we all agreed she'd basically been asking for it and we moved on, unaffected. Nothing mattered except chasing our next drink. Why had I wasted so many years being sensible? Why hadn't I spent every weekend like this? Greenie marched on up front, Tommy and Finn a bit behind him, singing, with me and Smith hanging back.

Smith's pretty quiet most of the time, hardly says anything, but as we staggered through the dark main street he whispered, *You know my favourite part? Tipping BIG. There's nothing like watching their eyes light up when they realise you've put a week's wages in their pants. They try and hide it, sure, but they can't.* That night we sat up later than the others, smoking and talking. *I work hard,* said Smith. I live in a boring suburb. *I look at TEETH for a living — when I was a kid I wanted to be Superman, you know? Now I can't even see my own kids without written consent. So if I want to come and have fun, no-one's gonna make me feel bad. I don't hurt anybody. Besides, the girls out here, mate, they're NASTY. They ask you to do the filthiest things. And the stuff they want you to say while you're doing it… It's like they hate themselves.* He grinned. *I fucking LOVE it.*

We got up late on Saturday, ate, then hit the bars and clubs again. In the evening Finn took us to that fetish club — I swear, I've never seen anything like it in my life. It felt like we were on a different planet. A better planet, worth living on, where guys like us were kings. And yes, before we left I did check out the toilets. Then we went back to the suite and Greenie got tied to a chair. We played music, more gutter porn on the tv on mute while we poured bottles of dirt-cheap spirits down his throat. The Saturday had started off like Friday, but we were all still drunk from the night before so it got messy, fast. We could hardly believe it but nobody at the hotel complained. We threw beer bottles out of the window, pissed onto the pavement, and even bought coke in the reception area from a taxi driver calling himself Dave (but who was really called something else — Radko, or something like that). He smelt money and gave us his phone number, promising he could get us anything we wanted, anytime. Apparently the locals expected this kind of thing. Tommy said the area was becoming the new hotspot for stag weekends, the government were encouraging it, and even the receptionists would do what you liked as long as you slipped them an incentive. *Serious,* he said. *There's like, no moral code here.* Later on Greenie dared Finn to ask this poor thing behind the desk how much she'd want for a blow job and I swear to God she considered it, looking Finn up and down, all silent, like she was working out whether she'd be able to live with herself if she said yes. I went back to talk to her later. *High shpirits,* I said, slurring my words. *Nuffin more. Shorry about that. Finn'sh a sholicitor you know. Divorsh, mainly. He'sh good. Hey, I'll get you hish card. In cashe you ever need it.* The last thing I remember was phoning Dave and asking what he meant by being able to get us *anything.* How about a giraffe? A clown? A corpse? Eventually, he hung up.

We woke late Sunday morning with killer hangovers, checked out, left bags in the lock up and crashed out on sofas in reception. After a while, conversations started up about ways to waste time until our flight home in the early evening. *What do you say we sample some local culture?* said Smith, who'd disappeared at one of the strip clubs the night before and only surfaced an hour ago, wearing dark sunglasses. Greenie cut in, *Not sampled enough already?* and a dirty laugh rippled round the group. But no-one had any better ideas, and no one could face more booze. So we set off walking through the city, Tommy leading with map in hand. There was an old church apparently. A market the receptionist had told us was 'quite good'. *A place the guilty can buy presents for their girlfriends,* said Greenie, and Tommy coughed. *What goes on in Vegas...* he said. *Know what I mean, boys?... Not that this dump is anything like fuckin'Vegas...* We were all tired but Greenie was still upbeat. *Come on, we might find some treasure!* I couldn't tell if he was joking, but on any other weekend I would have been pleased to find myself in some strange European city with a few hours spare to explore, so I said, *Sure. Fuck it. Let's go.*

After a couple of wrong turns and a lot of walking we arrived at the church, and it really was impressive. Under the vast gothic entrance there was a message translated into English on a sign by the door. Most of the words had letters missing, but it was still possible to make out the meaning. The building had been pieced together, it said, *thanks to the money, dedication and hard work of people from all over the world, to celebrate the liberation of this proud nation from the Ottoman Empire at the end of the 19th Century.* Never again, thought the labourers, as they heaved brick upon brick, stone upon stone, would this place be ruled by outsiders. Future mistakes would be their own; future glories too. It was built in hope of what a new century might bring. I stood back to take in the whole building, brain still fuzzy with last night's mixed drinks.

The beers that started it all. The shots that finished it. I took a photo on my phone to show Heather when I got home.

We decided to go in for a look around. In the echoed near-darkness of the old building there was a real sense of that haunting feeling you only get in some Eastern European prayer houses — ones that have survived crimes so bad no one talks about them. A mournful priest to our right with a long dark beard and black robe looked like he'd wandered in, lost, from a different century. He swayed in front of high, thin candles, muttering underneath his breath, a guide nearby explaining the history of the city to a group of tourists who took snaps of the stained glass windows as she talked. Standing in the centre of the floor, looking upward into the bright light above, I imagined what it must have been like for the builders, proudly putting the final touches to the ceiling. Perhaps I could take a break from work and live here for a while. Maybe Heather would come with me. Would she understand if I told her I knew what to do with my life, and this was it? Standing in this spot, looking up? I began to feel sick.

When I joined the others outside the church, I noticed a market in front of us. It was modest, just twenty or thirty small stalls stretched out on either side of a path. But it seemed like a kind of heaven. At the first stall Finn called me over to show off an antique he wanted to buy. He held up a fine, perfectly operating pocket watch on a chain. *Nice,* I said. *You sure it's not fake?* But Finn just said, *This is IT, man. This place. You know?* I felt I knew what he meant. After a little haggling over the price he bought the watch and chatted to the stallholder for a while. Just being curious. Finding out how many years the market had been going. Whether he'd been busy that morning. How long he'd lived here. Finn played the part of the interested, respectful tourist every bit as well as the arrogant arsehole who'd said over dinner on Friday, *I'm not leaving this shithole until I've seen some local tits!*

At the next stall a selection of knives were laid out in rows, ranging from blades the size of my index finger to the size of my arm. Most were blunt, but in amongst them was a shiny one in good condition. *Not interested,* said Smith, seeing me look. *Never been used. Display case* only. Next to the display knife was a much smaller specimen, which looked like it could no longer slice a tomato. *Now there's a battle knife,* he said. *I wonder how many people that one killed.* I stepped in closer to examine the little weapon, and found it hard to believe it had ever been dangerous. At the base, in the centre, was a darker blotch than the light grey surrounding. I thought I could make out an emblem, but that had worn away years ago. Probably in the hand of the man who held it.

The third stall was a better-stocked version of the first two. It had knives but also other trinkets too, and piles of pictures just lying on the table, loose. *Good, good,* said the stall holder, pointing. *Look.* So I picked up a batch and flicked through a series of old black and white photographs. These were mainly posed portraits of aristocratic families, but also some written-on postcards and a few official government-issue images from as far back as the 1930s, including, strangely, one of Adolf Hitler pictured in front of a black background, as if in a studio set up especially for the event. I'd only ever seen images of this man looking ugly, or crazed, or sinister — but here he looked like a handsome winner. I returned the batch. At the back of the stall a collection of army uniforms were hanging on a rail, originating from several European countries, and several eras. Some of these uniforms were sets, others just a pair of ripped trousers, or a dirty helmet. I was beginning to think I wouldn't find anything for Heather after all.

At the very front of this stall, between two ordinary sets of candlesticks, I was drawn to a shiny silver hip flask, more beautiful than anything in my collection. The five Olympic rings were imprinted on the side, and underneath was the label: *Berlin 1936.* At the bottom was a dark grey circle with a swastika inside. I'd never seen anything like this before, in perfect condition. Could I buy it? Would I be able to get it out of the country? What if airport security noticed it? Would they believe I was just a collector? What if they put me in prison? *For sale, good price, for you,* said the stallholder, sensing my interest. *Where did you get these from?* I asked. *Austria,* he said. *We pick up in markets. For souvenir, yes? Original Nazi — seventy years old!* He kept talking but I just stayed looking at this hip flask, wondering who had owned it, for how long, and how it had come to be here, now, waiting to be picked up by me. Maybe it was never used. Maybe it was display case only, like the knife. Or maybe it had been the most prized possession of some soldier who needed a shot of courage before going into battle. I looked closely at the stallholder, and knew he had no idea what it was worth.

I'd forgotten about the others, but looking round now I saw them at different stalls, inspecting some strange pieces as closely as I was. Finn and Smith were looking at items from the Communist era here. Greenie and Tommy were nearby looking at some coins, two or three old guns, another smiling fatherly face — Stalin this time, reclining at home. The dregs of every dead regime who'd conquered this country and sucked it dry were represented here at the market. Every one since the church was built. But it also attracted dictators from elsewhere. In amongst the Nazis and Communists was a clutch of old defunct money, laminated, with Saddam

Hussein looking out. The stallholders were as happy to sell a Nazi helmet as a Communist badge as an Iraqi note. No distinction was made between country or leader. All were shit. All were the same. Another stall sold a mix of Russian doll caricatures. Next to the other politicians were figurines of Tony Blair and Gordon Brown, each painted on a Union Jack background, grinning dumbly, just like Hitler and Hussein. Everyone was in the pot together. It was at that moment, looking at all the junk, that I was sure. I went back and bought the hip flask, checking the others weren't looking as I handed over the few paltry coins the stallholder asked for. Then I stuffed the thing deep into my jacket pocket, hand tight around the cold exterior.

I looked back at the church as the five of us walked away from the market. It looked like no one had been by to clean it in years. The whole area now looked like that — like someone had been meaning to tidy up for a decade or more but never quite found the time or the funds to finance it. On the church steps, old women with faces like crumpled tissues sold single, half-dead flowers to the odd pitying tourist; if the flowers were rejected, they dropped the act and just asked for cash. Once the place was out of view, Tommy said to Smith, *What did you think of that then?* And Smith surprised us all. *It makes me feel ill,* he spat. *They should be ashamed.*

The rest of the afternoon dragged. We were all exhausted so we went into a nearby hotel and watched the football — everywhere showed English games here, even the crap ones. Tommy spent ages on the phone to his fiancée, Smith kept going off to vomit and even Greenie said he was ready to go home. He was leaving for Dubai in five days and had lots to do. I kept my jacket on all afternoon, forgot about getting a present for Heather and didn't let go of my little container of history.

And I kept it, until last week. Twelve months unemployed had cleaned me out, so I had to sell off the whole collection. There's a big black market out there; the Nazi hip flask sold to some mug in South Africa and the money paid for return flights to Dubai. As I told Greenie, sitting in his plush apartment, stoned, overlooking the water and multi-coloured skyscrapers stretching off into the distance, I realised I had to look forward now. Soon I'd return home and begin again. Live clean. Live right. *But not quite yet,* he said. Then we went out on the town.

Todo lo que yo esperaba que me diera placer y que [...] me convenció para emprender el viaje me había decepcionado —., Pero fuera de esa decepción muy, he adquirido una educación inesperado

THERE'S ALWAYS ARIZONA

You put the earphones into your ears while looking for your keys. You find them in your jacket pocket, where you left them. Then you check your bag for the second time, count the papers inside, and zip it up. *That's me gone!* you say, standing in the bathroom doorway, not moving. *I'm not here now!*

Jennifer works nights and hasn't been to sleep yet. This is her midnight. She's in the bath, blowing at bubbles in her palm. *Sure you're not here,* she says back, reaching for the bottle of white wine. *I can see that. Don't let the nasty men eat you up, okay?* She swigs and returns the bottle to the floor. *Remember, they can't prove anything.* A silence. *And if they can,* she says, *we'll just move to Arizona. I hate it here anyway.* Jennifer has this way of talking. You can't always trace the tone.

What? you ask. *Where are we going?* You check the time. Maybe you should arrive early.

To Arizona! she says. *We can put a pillow over Auntie Joan's head. No one will notice. Besides, she's like, a million years old. She wants to die. And then there's the land...*

You smile. *I reckon I could be a farmer,* you tell her, stepping back into the hallway. *You'd look good in dungarees. But what would we do with the body?* You look at the clothes on the bedroom floor, the half empty cans, the ashtrays, and think about staying at home today.

You look back at Jennifer. She wiggles her toes, dips her head under the water and comes back up, a hat of white foam on her head. She says, *The body? Fuck it, I don't know, do I? We could bury her under the porch, or chop her up and feed her to the dog or something. We'll work it out! Daniel, we're supposed to be outlaws!*

I have to go, you call, closing the door behind you. *See you tonight. Or earlier.*

If you know Jennifer, she'll take another sip of wine, pick the phone up off the side and call her mother from the bath. She'll wonder what really happened last week. You've told her already, but you have this way sometimes. She can't always trace the tone.

You walk down the old spiral staircase, tie tied tight, newly-cleaned shirt smelling of detergent and still warm from a rare, brief clash with the iron. Your shoes are shined and buffed. The others in the office won't recognise you in a suit, but it doesn't matter. If you're gonna be saved, it's not smartness that'll do the saving. Right now, Greg is probably welcoming the guys from Head Office, the three of them planning their strategy over coffee, considering options. Or maybe Greg is showing them around the place, introducing them to a few of his office favourites, the ones he calls *my little stars,* by which he means *my little sellers.* Soon they'll all be sitting down in the boardroom, the three of them, using words like *protocol,* and phrases like *you've got to make an example haven't you?* while Andrea offers tea and old biscuits with a sigh. You can't think about that, or anything else. Why would anyone waste their time?

Instead, you pick your iPod out of your pocket, and scroll down the screen as you walk.

It's a short journey to the office. Which is usually a good thing.

Around this time of year, deep in winter, when days are short, you have friends who have to shower and shave when it's still dark outside. Your brother works twelve hours at a time, eight till eight. The woman in the flat opposite leaves at six every morning, travelling for two hours before sunrise. That's ten hours in blackness every week, all that time to think on the move, and another ten on the return journey. Too much thinking leads to mistakes. Once, in the hallway, you told a neighbour you could almost see your desk from your bedroom window, like it was a joke you could both share. She faked a smile while you told her you could put off getting up till half eight, sometimes quarter to nine, and *still* arrive early enough to make coffee before punch-the-clock time, slipping on your headset and making the first call of the day, all while still being effectively asleep. Now you think of this, it doesn't seem like it was such a clever thing to say. She's a manager of some kind. Jennifer said she was off with depression for months. What's wrong with you? Why don't you think about other people? Perhaps the panel will ask that.

Some mornings, when you're tired or hungover, you calculate how much you save in travel costs every week by living so close to the office. Then you work out how much you save per year, and it makes you feel warmer. This morning is different though. This morning you dream of a lengthy commute. A long walk, a bus, a train across the city. Enough time to wake up, think clearly, work out what the fuck you're gonna tell them. Just in case you decide to fight, or beg forgiveness. *Can I speak to the home owner please?* you said, as you did a hundred times a day, as you'd been doing six shifts a week for months. *Are you aware you could save up to 50% on your energy bill by switching to a different provider?* Still, this short walk down the hill, round the corner, across the main road and up the steps to the reception area — at least it's long enough to listen to one tune. As you step out onto the street, you realise you might not be making travel savings for much longer. Then you hit *SHUFFLE*, wondering what the gadget will choose. The world is in your ears.

In the first few bars, you recognise it.

You don't usually believe in omens. But now you wonder.

This song always has the same effect. The first notes open a valve in your chest that releases all the pressure inside your body, a valve that usually you can't even find, never mind manipulate. It moulds you into a new shape. The shape of a taller, thinner man, who's standing upright. Or a smaller, fatter one, reclining in a Jacuzzi, somewhere tropical. This morning the valve works fast and as the song builds you feel brighter, all that pressure seeping through your clothes and into the cold air around, spilling onto the pavement, the road. You breathe the pressure out, up, up, into the grey, away and over the tops of the tenements, thinking that maybe you were wrong. Maybe you can do this. The keyboards swell slightly, just slightly in your ears; that quick, faint arpeggio rising and falling, rising and falling, a sound almost too soft to be an instrument, and you briefly forget where you're headed. Then you remember again, thinking to yourself, *I'd like to die please, in the next few minutes. And I'd like this song to be played at my funeral.* For a moment, this is your only wish, and you imagine mourners wondering what it all means as they listen. Why you've chosen this sound as your final statement. You quicken your walk to fall in time with the music. The clipped rimshot of wood on metal is your heartbeat. You consider good ways to go, and think about how Greg would cope with never getting to complete the disciplinary process. It's almost worth closing your eyes and stepping into the traffic.

You reach the bottom of the road then turn the corner.

You said, *Yes, I know you already have a provider Mrs Pendleton, but what if I told you I could save you nearly seventy pounds?* On the other end of the line, she murmured, wanting to be polite, wanting you gone. She finally said, *How much?*

Thinking about Mrs Pendleton sets you thinking about writing a will. It makes you want to spell out your instructions. Everything to Jennifer. Everyone else can go fuck themselves. Where are they this morning? Where is the calm, clear advice of friends and family? The support? Why does the phone not ring? As you think about this, you feel the beginnings of something like a prickly rising heat at the edges of your being, pulling you tight. It's a light fluttering in the rib cage. A sickly feeling in the stomach. What if you get run over before arriving at work? What if you die and they give you a funeral like your father's? You imagine some placid, bovine Servant of the Lord, tweaking the speech he's been giving for decades, filling in the gaps where names need to be, talking about how really you were *a deeply spiritual person* who, though not a regular in the pews, was an *upright and moral citizen* who *lived by Christian values,* now somewhere in the ether, *being welcomed into God's eternal warm and loving embrace.* Thinking about God's eternal embrace, you feel your throat tighten, your breathing becoming restricted. You've got to be careful. You don't want to do anything which might end up killing you off before you've got the appropriate paperwork in order. Still, maybe it's worth living. There's always Arizona.

Something in you crackled. You thought of her standing there, trying to get rid of you, and you said, *Actually Mrs Pendleton, fuck it. Do you know what? Just fuck it. Fuck it all.* Mrs Pendleton didn't know what to say. Someone took the phone from her.

Even though nothing you need for this meeting can be found in your bag, you stop and check again. What are you looking for in there? The first verse of the song comes to an end, volume rising, the buzz and hum of one guitar pouring into your left ear as the siren wail of the other screams in your right. No one else you know has even heard of this band, and in a way that makes them yours. They're from another planet. Canada. You've never seen them on television or heard them on the radio. You don't know what they look like. They've been powering on, hitless, for a decade, singing songs about bitterness and bad credit and the power of rock 'n' roll. They're still playing clubs and fending off part-time jobs. They're still dreaming. This band says everything you want to say, better than you could ever say it. They forgive all your sins.

Mrs Pendleton, you said, before you started crying, not knowing it was no longer Mrs Pendleton you were speaking to, *Please, Mrs Pendleton, just put the fucking phone down.*

The song swoops and dives and urges you on.

People walk past you. Most are also listening to music through earphones, cocooned in their imaginations. Some faces you recognise. You wonder if you look different to them this morning.

As you up your pace, getting closer, closer to that boardroom — why go at all? why not just run? — the song moves into a chorus. It's pushing onward, but it sounds exhausted, the singer's voice bruised and cracked, the sound of years of bedding down in cheap hotels and on fans' bedroom floors. He's telling you, this man who is more of a success than you'll ever be, but less than he wants to be, about how his soul wants to sing a hateful song, but he's refusing to do it. Even though it's aching to get out. You think, these sounds are made by people, by everything those people have ever done, seen, lost. Then you think, maybe when you die, you don't want a funeral at all. Maybe you'll throw a party instead. No solemn speeches, no mourning, no wringing of hands or regrets and no casket. Really, if you think about it, this is a positive, hopeful sound you're listening to. It's a survivor's song. And after all, you're a survivor. So if you *do* die today, your mourners could be dancers, their black hats and coats turned into floral pattern shirts and dresses, tears of sorrow transformed into tears of joy, each person reaching for the skies, singing along to your favourite song, your brother telling a friend with a smile, *This is what Daniel would have wanted.* Then they'd go round in a circle and share their memories of you. Today, you're gonna survive. As you walk, you swell.

You imagine Jennifer scattering your ashes.

Then: your corpse being thrown out of a plane.

Then: ritual suicide at your desk.

Then: having a job you don't hate.

You cross the road at the lights, feeling strangely free, playing imaginary drums with your arms through the second chorus, not caring if anyone else sees, not caring what they think of you. Hitting the air feels like hitting Greg who will, by now, surely be aching for your arrival, the conversation with his superiors from Head Office now that bit more awkward, stilted, as the meeting approaches. The transcript of your crime will be typed and placed in front of each panel member, another copy typed by Andrea, for you, so you can't escape what you've said, every *fuck* circled and highlighted. Meanwhile, in the next room, rows of Greg's little stars try to forget what's happening to you as they pace through their lines, each call being recorded, while they search for that crucial next sale, pressing that bit too hard for a commitment so they can add another big tick to their sales figures and everyone can clap.

Greg sometimes writes down things he wants to say in advance. He might have written down *Do you know how much you scared Mrs Pendleton, Daniel? Do you think it's fun to take advantage of little old ladies? To attack the vulnerable in that way?* If he asks that, and if you don't run out of the room or break into tears, you hope you'll have the courage to remind him that taking advantage of little old ladies is part of your fucking job description.

It's halfway through the final chorus when you realise you might have misunderstood this music. Competing with the growl and rev of noisy morning traffic, the words seem muffled, the distortion doesn't have the same crunch you remember, you think there's a lyric in there that you didn't notice before, you focus on it, the final line of chorus could mean just about anything, and in that split second all certainty evaporates. You wonder what this new uncertainty might mean. Then your mind is wandering again, and you wonder if maybe the song is not about love or hope but actually just about money, about how the men in this band never had any of it, and how really they don't know if they can go on like this much longer. Suddenly the song sounds like a kind of defeat. The drums sound tired, the thump of the bass tom sounds weak, like it's been punctured then taped up to cover the holes. The guitars sound old and battered, the leads buzz. Vocals crackle into a smashed-in microphone. You imagine each band member trying to pretend they're somewhere else as they battle through this old tune one more time, maybe in front of a crowd of a thousand. Or twenty. Considering a career change. This song never used to sound like this. It must be you that's changed.

You turn the final corner.

I'm sorry Mrs Pendleton, you said, finally regaining your composure. *I'm sorry. You're probably just as well sticking with your current provider.* Her son spoke quietly into the receiver. *You should be ashamed of yourself.*

Jennifer is right. What you need is not old words; what you need is Arizona. You picture your arrival at Arizona Airport (you don't know what it's called), picking up a convertible at Arizona Car Hire (or whatever), and heading out onto the Arizona freeway, top down, hair blowing in the breeze with this song blasting out of the speakers. (You have no idea about the landscape in Arizona, which other states it borders, whether it has call centres and bosses called Greg.) It's another universe you're in here, where this band are popular and rich and the song is on the radio all the time. Next to you, Jennifer is in big red sunglasses, holding a pillow in her left hand, wielding it like a hammer and saying, *It's what Auntie Joan wants. And besides, what can she do with a hundred acres?* The two of you are kissing deep kisses, holding hands. You'll never see that old office again, or any office again. From now on, each day will be a steady climb up a mountain which is satisfying but challenging, manageable, with no unsteady passages or loose rocks. One day you'll reach the top of the mountain and laugh about the time you were fired for crying and swearing down the phone to a stranger. *Do you remember that?* you'll say to Jennifer, laughing. *Can you really believe that was us?* You won't hate Greg, though the hate is in you. You won't hate anyone at all.

As the last notes of the outro fade to nothing, you notice you've arrived at work. You switch off the music. It feels like hours since you left home. Standing outside the office block, looking upward, you hesitate, then check your bag one final time — for what, you don't know. Then you text Jennifer. The message reads: *ARIZONA?* You step forward, buzz the office intercom, Andrea says, *Is that you, son?*, and you answer, *Dead man walking. Is the executioner here?*

Her laugh sounds like a cough.

She lets you in.

The reply comes through quickly, and you read it as you're climbing the stairs.

It reads: *REALLY?*

Tout ce que je m'attendais à me donner la joie et qui [...] m'a convaincu d'entreprendre le voyage m'avait déçu —. Mais hors de cette déception même, j'ai acquis une éducation inattendu

DO ALL THINGS WITH LOVE

My shirt is clinging to me. A thick line of sweat runs from my shoulders downwards, following the straps of my rucksack. Still, despite the heat, and the sweat, and having no idea what street or even district I'm in, I walk down this road with no apparent end, towards no place, thinking mostly of my blessings. My heavy suitcase feels weightless. The handle is wet and the whole thing glides as if the wheels are enjoying movement. Eventually I'm going to have to get out the map, but for now I think, *Just walk*. Canada is a highly developed first world nation and I'm on a main road in a busy part of Toronto — a clean, safe city whose streets have been planned by someone with the good sense to use a grid system. The old Harry Moore would have reached straight for the Lonely Planet. The new one prefers to let it sit in the bag.

Each time someone walks past me I smile and nod, sometimes gesturing up to the sky as if to say, *How about this weather then?* Hilary used to complain that in situations like this I act like an unelected ambassador for tourists everywhere. Operating in exaggerated gestures, grin fixed, seeking approval. As if a gang of other suitcase-wielding travellers are, at that exact moment, going about the same streets as me, stealing, committing arson, slaughtering then devouring all the newborns they can find. In Hilary's last days she said she didn't recognise me anymore. She claimed she'd happily slit her throat to spend a single night with the Teddy Boy biker she married, who couldn't care less what other human beings did, thought or said. But James Dean is long gone, it's nice to be nice, and Hilary's not here with me in this gorgeous country, with all this space and greenery and sun that makes me feel twenty years younger. So I can smile and nod if I want. I can even say hello. People are not monsters. Most say hello back and leave our brief exchange with the sense that, despite everything, we are not lone birds in the sky.

A few streets later I stop and lift my suitcase up onto a bench which has a sign on it reading: *FOR AMANDA.* No dates. No surname. I run two fingers over the brass plaque. I'm thirsty. I can't remember which pocket my water bottle is in so I prop my rucksack on top of the suitcase and begin to search the pouches. Every one feels like it might have water in it. None of them does. But just as I'm imagining abandoned bottles all over today's trail — the airport terminal, the bus, the last intersection — I notice some blood on my arm. A tiny little dot, as small as the first half-drop of rain in a light afternoon shower. This occupies my attention until I look down and see that, apart from the area covered by my rucksack straps, my white shirt is no longer white.

So I've been at the café since seven, answering emails and touching up this damn report. I'm the only customer for the first hour and the staff set up for the day around me. It's cool, they're used to it.

Whenever I finish a job I tick it off on the morning's list with my big red pen. Every half hour I break off to chat to the fresh-off-the-boat Italian boys behind the counter, then I go back to work. At nine I turn off the laptop and put it out of sight. I read the *Business Times* over fruit, yoghurt and yet more jet black coffee, which smells like almonds and reminds me of my mum. New boy Silvio serves my drink with a smile, wagging a finger close to my face. *Too much workie workie,* he says. *You no want a nice magazine to read?* As I watch that tight ass slink away, I think, *I'm pretty damn sure he never works too hard.* Around nine thirty I fold up my paper, leave the usual tip and wave goodbye for the day. Next I stop in the grocery store for milk, tampons, toilet roll. Nothing sexy. My first meeting isn't until ten thirty, and Christ knows some of us put in the hours. There's no reason to rush, right?

When I pull off Queen Street West onto Ossington I'm sliding on my sunnies and walking slower than usual cos hey, I'm early, and it's hot. I head up for a while, thinking I'm gonna cross by Hamilton Park, waiting on the lights. Seems like everyone is either on the phone, or they're checking their phone. Mine hasn't rung since I turned it on. The lights change, I start to cross, and then I see this touroid walking my way. Pacing right on through the middle of the traffic, wandering left and right, like maybe he's a ghost, or no one's told him cars can be pretty dangerous, you know? Anyway, somehow he avoids getting crushed, and the closer he gets, the colder my skin feels, and pretty fast I get to thinking, *what's happening here*? He's getting closer, and my eyes are watering. Maybe I need a day off to catch up on some sleep — shit, maybe I need a *lifetime* off — but he seems *like a ghost*, this guy. Like he's *ageless*. Well, whatever he is, whoever he is, this one's got my attention. Fuck it, let's say he's sixty-five.

So he's floating along, this maybe-sixty-five-year-old ghost-touroid, looking around as if he's just arrived in paradise and can't believe his luck. He's looking at the park like the old dudes on the benches are cherubs and the grass is made of gold. He's...

This guy... It's like he's *never seen a park before*. We cross and he gives me this *look*, tilts his head up to the sky and says, *Hello friend!* Well, I just spill out *Hello friend* back (I know, it must have been the shock) and then BOOM, he's passed me. I turn around to see what he's gonna do next. Sometimes I just *sense*. I watch, as he stops at the bench, dumping his case on it, looking in his bag. I pull out my cell. Pretend to send a message. Then he turns around. And what I can see in front of me is a guy in a suit, bleeding to death.

Stay calm, I tell myself. It's no good getting angry. Besides, there's no one to be angry at. It's only me, my bags and this redness. So I stop. I wait to feel a rush or a spasm or a sting of some kind. Something that's going to confirm that yes, my leg has fallen off. But this realisation doesn't come, all my limbs remain firmly attached, and I'm in no discomfort whatsoever. Where on earth is this coming from? I examine my shirt to see if the damp patch is darker in one place or another. It's not. It's strangely uniform, this colouring. My situation is not ideal but, like old Helmuth Von Moltke the Elder used to say, *No battle plan survives first contact with the enemy*. And you don't stay Chief of Staff of the Prussian Army for 30 years if you don't know your chips! So when my own battle plan needs a rethink, I act fast. I take off my suit jacket, then my shirt, then I start looking for places this madness might be originating from. *First weigh the considerations, then take the risks.* That's another of Helmuth's greatest hits. Next, I drop my trousers.

Swear to fucking God, right in the middle of Ossington. First thought was maybe he's not a touroid at all. Maybe he's another one escaped from the crazy house. Wandering the streets of Toronto, pants round his ankles, looking for his dead dog or some shit. Hoping to get picked up by aliens and carried back to Mars.

The redness has gathered slightly in three or four places, but none of these have a cut near them. I'm still leaking, and I begin to imagine the blood pooling at my feet. Rising steadily, filling up the street, turning into a red ocean and drowning all the citizens of this fine country where the sun shines and strangers say, *Hello friend!*

I begin searching for a packet of tissues. Surely to God then I'll find, out of a process of elimination if nothing else, where this bleeding is coming from. It's going everywhere. It's dripping onto the near-white pavement. If there's a heaven, and Hilary is in it, and if you can look down from there to here, she's certainly shaking her head right now. She's watching me, swearing like a soldier and telling the dead person next door all about the jazz singer who proposed to her in the mid-'70s, back when we were having *one of our lean years*. She's wondering about the other lives she could have had, hanging off the arm of a pioneering doctor, or some kind of rebel prince. Anyone but a fucking sales rep. Meanwhile I'm down here with my head falling off my shoulders. If I'd checked in straight away instead of going walkabout I could be bleeding safely in private right now, in front of a hotel mirror, onto a towel I'm not responsible for washing. But no. Free Harry knew so much better.

I finally find that bottle of water, consider pouring it over my chest, then decide against. I'm not an animal am I? This episode has lasted minutes, not decades. And besides, it's probably best to just drink, hydrate, keep looking. *Keep calm and carry on* and all that. I'm sure I have tissues somewhere, but they need to be found fast. The world stops spinning for no one! Blood runs down my arms and drips into the rucksack, blotting my diary, my camera, the notebook Hilary gave me. My hands are sticky, the creases now a web of fine red lines. There's blood under my thumb nail. It's begun to appear in spots on my legs. I empty the whole rucksack onto the street. My face flushes red. There's nothing else for it.

So right there, this guy, who looks like
a tomato with hands, is almost down to
his Garden-of-Edens, right? He's about
to open his suitcase, and I'm thinking *No!*
If there's ANYthing in that case worth
keeping it'll be fucked. And I have to be
the martyr, right? So I'm running, calling
out, *Sir! Sir, stop!* Like I'm his Alfred and
he's Bruce fuckin WAYNE or something.
I haven't called anyone Sir since my
waitressing days. And as I'm running and
talking like a butler or waitress or whatever,
I'm reaching for the toilet paper in my bag.
For a second I think, oh man, an omen! But
no, I just happen to have come direct from
the grocery store. No cosmic magic here.
The guy stops unzipping the case halfway
and looks over. *Hello friend!* he says again,
standing up. Like he was waiting for me.
But this time I don't talk. I'm busy.

And before you know it I'm standing there in
my Harley Davidson boxer shorts with this
woman I've never met who's approached
me like a thirty-something angel bearing
Kleenex. She's refilling my rucksack, then
searching my body for wounds amongst
the patterns of spreading red. Then she's
wiping me down. I offer to do it myself but
she's insistent: it'll be quicker if she charges
ahead, and anyway, I'm likely to just keep
dripping everywhere. So when she tells me
to raise my arms, I raise my arms. When she
tells me to step onto the grass I do so, loose

belt buckle rattling behind me. She's used half a toilet roll already; damp pink ribbons of the stuff are collecting around our feet.

Despite everything, my temperature's rising. I'm looking around, trying not to look, not to think the obvious — but to be fair to the good people of Toronto, they don't do much. They look, smile, think about offering to help, then don't. They've seen worse no doubt, and I don't make a fuss either. Like Theodore Roosevelt used to say: *Do what you can, with what you have, where you are.* And Teddy was — still is — a man worth listening to. What I can *do* here is what I'm told, what I *have* is help, and *where I am* is earth, which is nothing more than a smallish, semi-environmentally-threatened planet in a galaxy of many others. All of which is fine, so long as you don't think about it too much. Looking around as the stranger wipes me, I notice this street is wide and lined with trees. This whole area is drenched in warm light. All this seems peaceful, and I consider changing my return flight. *Everything's gonna be okay,* says the stranger. And she's oddly convincing.

She keeps me talking by asking questions. Should she call an ambulance? Do I feel faint? Do I have a blood disorder? Have any family members suffered with such things in the past? What about my heart — do I feel like I'm having a heart attack? I answer each of these questions steadily: *No, No,*

No, No and No. I'm thinking: *what would Hilary make of this?* They say people don't care about each other. They say this world of ours can't be fixed. Well how would they explain this, eh? How would they explain it? The woman tells me to lift my arms up higher, she's trying to get to my armpits. There's blood dripping from the hair. And then, just as I'm almost clean, she says, *Aha!*

No shit, this thing is smaller than a pin head. If it wasn't leaking you wouldn't be able to trace it. It's a teensy dot between the top bones of the ribcage. It's nearly not there. But every time I cover it or wipe it, the little fucker starts to leak again. The blood is coming fast. First I touch the pin head with my finger and see it's a slightly raised lump, maybe a capillary or something. In the moment, I'm thinking about AIDS. I'm thinking about all the ways I might die after touching this man. All the ways he might die. We might be killing each other just by standing in this place, doing this thing. Sometimes I think all Toronto goes about in gamer mode, imagining hitmen, super-zombies and world-threatening epidemics on every block. Turns out, when it comes to small holes on the chests of strangers, I'm exactly the fuckin same as all the other dumbasses in this city.

OK so I ball up a big piece of tissue, the fattest ball you can imagine, right? I press the middle of it onto the pin head bit, saying,

HOLD. He holds. Which gives me time to clean the rest of him without distractions. It takes forEVER, but Praise the fuckin Lord, after maybe ten long minutes, we're finally making progress. After all that red, this guy, he's so white in places he looks more like a boiled egg than a human being. While I'm rubbing all he keeps saying is, *Thank you, thank you* and *You're so kind* and *The people here! You're all wonderful!* He's got this old Teddy Boy haircut, a medallion round his neck, and he's wearing a bracelet that reads: *PROPERTY OF HILARY MOORE.* He looks like he hasn't slept in days. Between my feet, I can see the grass is changing colour.

Sometimes she says, *Press harder.* She rolls her eyes and says: *You call that hard?* My hand aches from holding this ball to my chest, and for a while I can't think of anything except how much I'd like to remove it. But then she calls out, *DONE!* and begins to clean herself. I still press, only softer now. I pull my trousers up and attempt to buckle my belt with one hand. Then I chance it, taking the damp clutch of paper off my chest for a moment. A thin red trickle dribbles down towards my belly button. I return the toilet roll and say, *It's not stopping is it?* She thinks for a few seconds. She says, *Let's sit. I like to eat here some days.*

After another few minutes I lift the towel again, with the same result. More trickle, which has to be re-wiped. I say to her, *What if it goes on forever?* She smiles as if addressing a child. *Nothing goes on forever,* she says. *Now let me think.* And that's when her face changes. Her eyes open wide and she's saying *fuck fuck fuck* underneath her breath. Perhaps she repeats the word twenty times, and I nearly get down on one knee right here at the bench, bloody fingernails or none. This woman with eyes like deep, clear pools of water and a filthy mouth is probably thirty years younger than me. She'd certainly refuse my advances. Such things only happen in bad Hollywood films and the worst kind of pornography. But marriage is an institution that suits me, and like John M. Richardson Jr says, *When it comes to the future, there are three kinds of people: those who let it happen, those who make it happen, and those who wonder what happened.* There's no doubt in my mind. It's about time I switched category.

> After being so early, so fresh, and so ready to kick ass, I'm gonna be late for my ten thirty.

It was the first word I heard Hilary say, in the bar where we met. I remember the barman asked her to watch her language. Well, my wife knew her mind. She advised the barman to have intercourse with himself, and it was then I decided to say hello.

Fuck fuck fuck. My hands are a mess, I'm sweating, and I haven't even called the office yet. I'm sitting here, sinking into the bench, and I think maybe they could do without me for an hour or two. Maybe I don't need to go in at all. I look at the touroid, who's looking into the distance.

Hilary would have liked this spot.

As I look at him, I think about shoring up the Davis account, my pile of paperwork and the unanswered emails in my inbox. I think about my Mom, and the last time I actually saw her, the market research on my desk, and the looks the secretaries give me whenever I ask them to do something. Then I think about how the guys from Head Office talk when they're asking ME to do something. How they change their minds just to show me who's in charge. Then I think about this space, my own corner of the city. And then I can't think of anything at all.

She weeps quietly.

To be fair to the old dude, when I have my freak out, he doesn't make a big deal.

The tears don't last for long, and when they stop, she's rid herself of something. She's ready now.

He gives me back some tissue he hasn't bled on yet. When he says, *There there,* in that really European way, it's like he's really making it better. I dry my eyes, take a deep breath, then phone Annie. In my usual even-tone office voice I say *I have an emergency which demands my immediate attention.* I ask her to reschedule my morning meetings. She'll do it. No questions, no weird tone. And a few seconds later I'm sitting there, cell still in my hand, looking up at the small white clouds in with all that blue, wondering, *what would really happen if I didn't go into the office ever again?* The clouds look so thin, so delicate. They've got so much work to do, holding themselves together. It's amazing they don't fall apart and drop right out of the sky. For a few seconds I forget I'm with another human being.

She asks my name.

His name is Jeffrey.

She tells me her name is Amanda. Next thing I know, I'm talking.

Turns out Jeffrey's wife died a week ago. They'd been married, like, *a hundred years.* First thing he did was retire. Second thing, catch a plane out here. No plans. No idea why, except he'd promised her he wouldn't sit around the house and wait to join her.

I'm sticking to facts. Dates. Places. I'm being breezy.

It's tragic. The guy is obviously in pieces.

Like I tell Amanda, it wasn't sudden, and we talked about what would happen afterwards. I promised Hilary dignity: no beating my chest with my fists. No ritual suicide on Allison Close. No tears for the neighbours. But the things in our home, in my head. I wonder if they'll ever let go of me. In Toronto, or anywhere. I mean, when your wife is everything, and everything is her, why would anyone wish that away?

It looks like he's gonna pass out or something. But then he pulls it back and says, *This bench. It's dedicated to you?* I answer, *Another Amanda. But sometimes I wonder.*

I smile. I daren't check my chest again. I think, *what if it really is my heart?*

Then I have an idea. I say to Jeffrey, *Let me take that suitcase. Do you think you can make it to your hotel?* He answers me like I've just asked him to part the Red Sea and he's only just figured out he's Moses. He thinks, breathes out hard and says, *I don't know where we are, Amanda. And I don't know where the hotel is. But with the Lord's help, I can try.* Is he serious? He stands. He looks pretty steady. Actually, he looks OK. And it's about now I think to myself, *why the hell didn't I just keep walking?* But he's so damn grateful. The address of his hotel is written in his guide book. It's six blocks away. Maybe Jeffrey isn't so lost after all.

The shirt is ruined. She tells me to throw it in the bin. But she wants me to put something around my shoulders to cover myself up, which I do, with one hand, all the while holding tissue onto my chest, only ever pulling away for a moment or two. She offers to help again, but a man has his limits. *Please*, I say. *No more.* I pick a jumper out of the suitcase and wrap it round my shoulders. My stomach is still exposed.

Sure, people will still think I'm walking with a crazy man, but at least one that's making an effort to *cover up* his crazy.

As we're walking, Amanda tells me she's lived here all her life. She shows me where she used to play as a child. She points out some of her favourite places, recommends the best spots for coffee, for food, gives me tips on where to avoid. She's talking fast and loud about this city. The spirit of the place. As we turn a corner she points up at a flat above a restaurant and says, *My cousin lives there. I should visit.* Then, almost so quiet I can't hear, she says, *I dedicated the bench to myself about three years ago, after my husband*

*died. Asked for it to face my apartment. How
lame is that?* I sway a little, she sees this and
secures her arm through mine, pulling me
closer. I tell her I'm fine. Which I really am.
I wonder whether the blood will wash off
my bracelet.

I ask him what he's doing in Toronto but he
just says, *I only arrived this morning.* Like
that answers my question. Like he wanders
the world waiting to see what happens next.
Who are you? I ask him, laughing. *What do
you even do?* Well, he just smiles and says,
*My dear, these days I do whatever I please.
My working days are done.* Then he offers
his arm and says, *Shall we go to see the
Wizard?* Slow and steady, I slip my hand
through, wheeling the suitcase behind us
with my other arm. Jeffrey grins like a boy.
He whistles for a while then says how much
Hilary loved the movies. I say something
about the Tin Man and the Lion, just to
keep him talking, you know? He keeps
telling me he's fine but he must think I'm an
asshole. Fingers clamped around his sticky
arm, my shoulder leaning in, I make sure
I'm holding him up.

We must be getting closer. It feels like we've
been walking for years. I close my eyes as
Amanda leads me, and I concentrate on
what the hotel lobby might look like. The
faces of the staff on reception. I think of
how soft the carpet in my room might feel

under my bare feet, and tell myself not to
think too big. Like Honest Old Abraham
Lincoln used to say, *The best thing about the
future is it only comes one day at a time.* And
all I have to do today is stop this bleeding.

> We turn a corner and see his hotel up
> ahead. All this time, Jeffrey's been holding
> the tissue over the spot with one hand.
> When we get to the reception desk and he
> lets go, we wait for the red to start again.
> But nothing. Maybe he's all bled out.
> I think about giving him my card or writing
> my number on a piece of paper. We both
> laugh. We can't believe it's really stopped,
> this bleeding. It's the greatest thing.

Oh, wow, I say. *Really. Oh my Lord.*

> His face is bright and full of colour. He looks
> at the palm of his hand, like the answers to
> all our questions are hidden in there.

I hold out the hand, I want her to see. She
looks at it. She keeps on.

> And without looking up I say, *You know
> where to find me.*

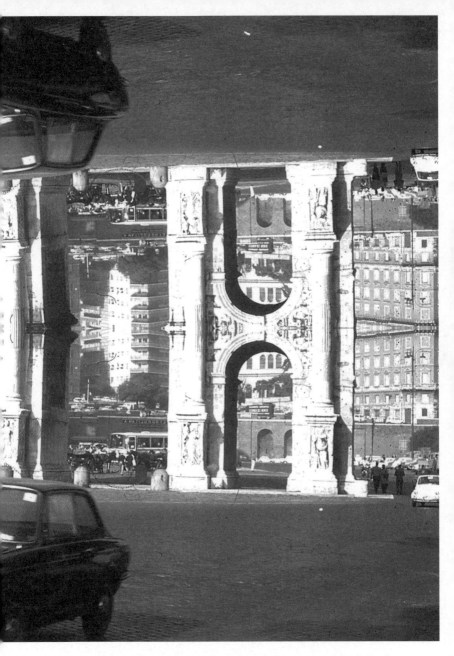

Alt, hvad jeg havde forventet at give mig glæde, og som [...]
overtalt mig til at foretage rejsen havde skuffet mig –. Men
ud af denne meget skuffelse, har jeg erhvervet en uventet
uddannelse

ORIENTATION #1

Visitors will find the Tivoli[1] easily. This 170-year-old landmark — described on its official website as *a unique mix of amusement park, dining area and performance venue* — is conveniently situated in Center (the area also known as K, or Indre By) and is clearly signposted on surrounding streets. Tivoli is prominently advertised on the Top Attractions page of visitcopenhagen.com (where you can source things to do under categories like Gay, Climate Friendly and Kids), and also in the many paperback guides available for a price which can surely not be sustained in this age of affordable data roaming. Chances are, Tivoli's entrance is only ten or fifteen

---

[1] The Danish Tivoli was originally called Tivoli and Vauxhall. It was named after the Jardin de Tivoli in Paris (which was, in turn, named after the Tivoli near Rome), and also the Vauxhall Gardens in London, England. 'Tivoli Gardens' is also a term used to refer to a community in Kingston, Jamaica.

minutes' walk from your hotel. So get there and get in the queue. It's very straightforward to find.

What you may find less straightforward is the reason you are in the Tivoli at all. Indeed, even at the moment you suggested a visit to your partner, friends or children, you may have been unable to remember why you chose this place over any other number of attractions in this City of Towers, such as the ruins of Bishop Absalon's 12th Century Castle, or the ever-popular Carlsberg Brewery. It's not like you knew the history of the Tivoli. You're not planning to ride the rollercoaster. Some of the visitors in the queue with you may say they always wanted to come here; others may blame Highlight Syndrome, the phenomenon by which tourists are drawn to already-popular sites, creating a self-perpetuating escalation in visitor numbers. Still others may more honestly ask, *Isn't this what everyone does?*

Denmark is a land rich in culture and heritage; many believe the site known as København was founded in the late Viking age, so there's history in these streets. In 1658 the city withstood a furious assault led by the Swedish King Charles X (1622-1660). In 1728 it burned to the ground and had to be completely rebuilt. The same happened in 1795. It's rarely taught in British schools but Nelson exploded some of Denmark's finest ships here in 1801, widely considered the famous Admiral's hardest-fought victory, and in 1807, the British subjected Copenhagen to what many now call the first terror bombardment of a civilian population. And that's not mentioning defeat by the Prussians in 1864, where Denmark lost one fifth of itself to Prussia — or occupation by the Nazis in more recent times. So Danes are tough, they've survived more than a little domination by larger neighbours, and if you reach out to Dr Bo Nielsen, a distinguished local Professor who happens to be walking past the Tivoli at this exact moment, you'll discover how much you don't know. Tap him on the shoulder. Ask him to prise open Denmark for you while the queue trickles forward. Bo can reach into cracks in the walls and draw out bunches of flowers. He can make a dish out of nothing. And isn't that what travel is all about? So fire him a question — what are you interested in? The Royals? Really? Okay, you're in charge. Whatever's your thing is our thing too.

Bo will explain that, though not as widely advertised as the British Windsors (who have a bigger budget and PR staff) or Juan Carlos's increasingly scandal-prone Spanish House of Bourbon, there is a fully functioning, respectable Royal Family here in Denmark, which is one of the oldest in the world. Since 1972 this has been led by Margrethe II (1940-), the first Danish Queen since the Act of Succession and subsequent referendum of 1953. She recently celebrated 40 years on the throne by first laying wreaths at her parents' graves, then riding from her birthplace, Amalienborg Palace, to the Rådhus (City Hall) in a gold carriage, escorted by the Regiment of Garderhusars. There she and other Royals attended a reception in Margrethe's honour and listened to a series of speeches about how great they all are. But you're probably not interested in dry constitutional details. If Bo focuses on them too much, ask him for more colour. More humanity. He won't be offended.

In a patient, clear, lilting accent, Bo will tell you that Margrethe II was raised in Denmark, before spending a year at boarding school in Hampshire and going on to study Prehistoric Archeology at Cambridge University. He'll tell you she speaks five languages and married a French diplomat. Otherwise, as any specialist will confirm, the Danish Royal family is riddled with Greeks.

They're also related to the Spaniards via Queen Sofia, a prominent member of the tongue-twisting Schleswig-Holstein-Sonderburg-Glücksburg dynasty. That sounds like a complicated family tree but it's all one big bowl of royal soup. Despite the French call for *Liberté! Egalité! Fraternité!* and Robespierre's guillotine-happy Terror, visitors to Copenhagen will note that over two centuries later, much of Europe's aristocracy is still alive and as incestuous as ever. It benefits from politicians who make them look positively democratic. Anyway, visit the Palace — as Bo will point out, it's enjoyable as a visual spectacle even if you're a republican or some kind of communist. It also hosts fine examples of Danish Rococo architecture. Ask Bo about that and his eyes will become torches; his wife prefers people to buildings and so he rarely gets the chance to talk on the subject. Once you've finished chatting, let Bo go on his way. He's already late for a meeting and has been too polite to say so.

Step back in line.

The queue has hardly moved. It's the busiest time of the week and the height of the season, so there's no point cursing. This was the only week you could get off work anyway — it's not like there was another option. Perhaps, while you wait to be admitted to Denmark's No.1 tourist spot, contemplate Bo's knowledge of his nation and consider what you might learn if you listened to these walls. And what about the others — is the Canadian family of five in the next line having a good time? Are the couple behind arguing? Even here you have to look hard to find anyone who is totally, truly joyful. So visitors to Copenhagen may wish to consider what makes *you* feel like a child on a swing.

Ahead in the queue, Richard from Johannesburg is gazing through the entrance at the resident Tivoli orchestra, who are playing the theme tune to Disney's The Little Mermaid. He's forty-three and not keen on instrumental music, but the notes have become words and now his skin is dancing. Like many visitors to Copenhagen, the imitation Little Mermaid statue in Langelinie[2] is Richard's next stop after here.

Though he's not aware of Hans Christian Andersen's 1837 fairy tale[3], or indeed the opera, and would probably dislike both, the sanitised Disney film is his daughter's favourite.

He's not seen her since the start of an access dispute but is planning to email his pictures to California where she now lives with her mother. This will be the start of a bad year — what the French would call a Série Noire — which will end with a conviction for trafficking South African girls to Europe, and bring a speedy end to the access dispute. He might not be a good guy, he might have body odour issues and an online dating profile full of lies, but if you forget the background noise and just look, Richard is simply a man, in the sun, enjoying an innocent sound rising from the bandstand and filling the whole park

---

[2] Sculpted by Edvard Eriksen, this was commissioned by Carl Jacobsen, son of the founder of Carlsberg, after he witnessed The Little Mermaid ballet performed at Copenhagen's Royal Theatre. The prima ballerina, Ellen Price, modelled for the head of the statue, while the sculptor's wife, who was prepared to model in the nude, provided the body. The statue in Copenhagen Harbour, which has been defaced many times, has always been a copy. The original is kept at an undisclosed location.

[3] The original 1837 story, titled Den Lille Havfrue, features cut out tongues, eternal damnation, betrayal and the little mermaid dancing in excruciating pain: fans of the Disney version wouldn't recognise it.

with colour. Soon the sounds will evaporate, as useless to him and to us as a sword made of sand. But for now Richard is a singing pitchfork. And what's so wrong with that? You can see demons everywhere in this world, but you'll never smile in your sleep.

Actually, this wait is ridiculous.

Look to your left. See that door peeping open? That's a Security entrance. The staff are paid badly and poorly motivated here, so it's easy to ghost through, and besides, the entrance price is a joke.

Step away from the queue.

Visitors to the city sometimes called Københavnstrup[4] will notice as you duck under the Security Only sign and swim towards the crowds that it's party time in the Tivoli. It's always party time! Here, excitement is continuous and consequence-free. There are over twenty restaurants and many bars. The entertainment is world class and it's all laid out for you: it couldn't be easier. Perhaps you find it relaxing to watch fish? If so, you can visit the aquarium and follow the feeding timetable; you've missed the sharks at 1300 but the seahorses are at 1500, piranhas at 1600 and the octopus, a real favourite with the little ones, is at 1700. After that you can take in a ballet at the Pantomime Theatre or a classical piece at the Concert Hall. It's Friday, which means Fredagsrock, and the cream of Danish music. All tastes are catered for — but perhaps you'll get more from your visit if you step away from the crowd. Yes, this way. Behind this bush. Shh. See those two men over

---

[4] This is a derogatory nickname used by Danes who are not from Copenhagen. It translates as 'the little unimportant city of Copenhagen'.

there? At the outside tables, the bar next to the ice cream parlour? Come on, come closer. Listen in.

Meet Hans, 29, and Daniel, 27. Hans has been single for five years, and struggling with manic depression for ten. Daniel hasn't stopped shaking since he left home. He's been single for five days, since his relationship with Jennifer finally snapped and she returned to her mother, in tears. Both men are drinking cold beers in the sunshine. Both got EasyJet flights for the price of a family meal at the Tivoli, they both came alone, and became friends late last night, meeting at a strip club bar populated by Romanian, Russian and Thai girls who feed off the sex tourists, responsibly wiring money home every month to their families. These girls could have told Hans and Daniel something about sacrifice if only they'd asked a question or two — but they only wanted to talk about themselves. How women treated them. How they'd given up on love. How they were here because they'd run out of hope.

Hans and Daniel drank in the club for hours, one eye on the floor show, pouring their lives all over each other. At intervals they tagged, going through to a back room where different girls danced for them. These girls did their standard act, then pulled each man's head softly to their breasts and listened to them talk. They whispered *I love you* and rubbed up against their jeans before sending them back to the bar. Later on, their colleagues repeated the process. Hans and Daniel left with empty pockets, having discovered they were currently reading exactly the same book, and had come to this part of Denmark sometimes referred to as Djævleøen (Devil's Island)[5] for the same reason. This was evidence! The fates had brought them together! They resolved to remain friends for life, making their promise at 5.30am on a dark Copenhagen side street. It's lunchtime now, they haven't slept, and both men are still drunk.[6]

If visitors look closely between Hans and Daniel they'll notice that sitting face-up on their table there's a copy of the book they were talking about, *Affluenza* by Oliver James. This edition has a man and a woman on the cover, both elegantly dressed, both standing in a futuristic lift,

---

[5] This is another derogatory nickname used by some in Jutland for the whole of Zealand, of which Copenhagen is a part. These Jutlanders make no distinction between Copenhagen and the rest of the island, though West Zealand and Copenhagen are very different in nature.

[6] There is no point in visitors becoming distracted at this juncture by the Swedish teenager storming past the two men with her headphones in, mascara streaking down her cheeks and pretending to play the drums. She's wearing full goth uniform and is full up with music: *SOME PEOPLE'S LOVE ISN'T STRONG ENOUGH* she screams — and given her family background, she does have a point. Her tears are a flood. She has a bruise on her left cheek. She's run away from parents who are dining at a restaurant in the Tivoli and are done pandering to her tantrums. This girl has never been at ease and she never will be. Look into her future and see that no matter how many people try to help, she will never be reached. She will commit suicide in seven years' time. She can't help us in our quest, some people are just doomed I suppose — so why look even for a second? If you offered her a tissue, a hug, some advice, she probably wouldn't be interested. If you offered her money, she'd reject it. The reality is, some people are just happier being unhappy. Go on, return to Hans and Daniel.

looking like they've lost a bet.[7] In the book, the author argues that the more money human beings have, the less happy they are. Brazil, this is true. China, this is true. Australia — absolutely true. In seventeen case studies (some of which Hans skipped — he runs a business and doesn't have much spare time) James links happiness to earnings, to the GDP of a nation. People in these nations get a pay rise, they get depressed. They buy a big house, they yearn for the cramped terrace they were raised in with their sisters. They win the lottery, they notice old friends acting differently and soon start dreaming of suicide.

But it doesn't count for everywhere. Nearly, but not quite. Look, visitors to Copenhagen: the exception is all around you. In Denmark, it turns out, people are fairly happy, even though they have the crippling disadvantage of being rich. The book says so. The studies prove it. It's something to do with equality between the genders and paternity leave or whatever. So visitors might want to change that schedule of theirs and study these streets, the buildings, the laws and regulations of this country that create such a successful blend, instead of standing with all the other moneyed miseries and taking photographs of The Little Mermaid. Hoover up the smell here. Talk to people. Ask them how they live. This country is more

---

[7] Oliver James is a popular psychologist, also the author of *They Fuck You Up: How to Survive Family Life* (Bloomsbury, 2002), named after the famous opening lines of the Philip Larkin poem. *Affluenza: How to Be Successful and Stay Sane* (Vermilion, 2007) has since been followed by a sequel to *They Fuck You Up*, entitled, *How Not to Fuck Them Up*, (Vermilion, 2011). When Hans becomes a father this time next year, he'll buy it.

likely to leave you at ease in your own skin. That is, if you leave the Tivoli for a second and go see something real.

For the last eight hours, Hans and Daniel have been touring places they think will make them happy. The Tivoli was supposed to be one of them, and in the haze of the strip club the idea seemed funny — from one extreme to another, no? They got in early, before the queue grew arms and legs. They went on some rides, ate ice cream, saw a show. They laughed for a couple of hours. But now time is treacle, all they can see are ghosts, and discussing the book is making it worse. Daniel in particular is drinking hard, to wipe out Jennifer. Love's a hard thing to kill. So now, when Hans suggests a visit to Christiania, Copenhagen's famous free state where marijuana is effectively legal, Daniel agrees. He's never tried drugs, either hard or soft. He's a bit of a drugs prude. But stripped, hollowed and desperate to be someone else, he feels that now, when everything he feared losing has already been lost, he might as well get wasted — if only for something to do, and to escape the couples holding hands here. So Hans and Daniel get up, take the book and begin walking through the Tivoli. Follow them. They've no idea where they're going but who cares? *Affluenza* will surely be their guide in this city some call the Queen of the Sea. And it's not like they're in a rush.

If they'd looked up events in Copenhagen before arriving, Hans and Daniel might had a different adventure. At this exact moment they're walking right past a café which does the best schnapps and herring in Denmark, and for a reasonable price too. Only a short walk away is the Literaturhaus, where tonight Carsten will spin golden word webs for an audience who will fly out of the door afterwards, looking at the world anew. Not that Hans and Daniel are into this sort of thing but they could be spontaneous. They could join the tattooed, the pierced and the hooded at an underground electronica club at the next corner, dancing themselves happy till the early hours. But no, they haven't got past the obvious. As the two men wander across a road, almost getting run over, Hans says, *Maybe we should just throw all our money away.* He looks left and right, thinks about which direction to go in, then takes a guess. Slurring his words he says, *Then we won't be rich. And we'll be happy. How much have you got?*

Keep following, visitors to Copenhagen. See how, for a moment, Daniel is unable to answer. Hans might be living off a generous allowance from his father in a tidy apartment in Kreuzberg, but since losing his job, Daniel has been struggling to accept the idea that where he's from, it's the excess of money, not the lack of it, that's the problem. He says, *Actually mate, I'm nearly at my overdraft limit.* Then, *But yeah, why not?* Daniel raises both hands in the air, lets out a roar — *ON TO CHRISTIANIA!* — then falls. Hans drags him up and the two men stagger forwards, singing and linking arms as they walk, bathed in sunshine and, they imagine, the warmth of the Danish people. It might look dirty to you but if you asked both men, at this exact moment, they'd tell you: this is the cleanest they've felt in years. Yes, alcohol is a depressant, but it also gifts fleeting moments of joy.

Visitors to Copenhagen will need to keep their distance. Or else they'll spot us.

At this exact moment, Hans and Daniel and are only just realising they have come full circle, being almost back at the entrance to the Tivoli. They can see it up ahead. They realise the mistake they've made and at the exact same moment they crack up, unable to hold back how absurd this all is. Say what you like about these two but at least they're able to poke fun at themselves. They can't stop laughing, in fact. And they instantly give up on the idea of going to Christiania, at least for tonight. Watch them hug and laugh, long and deep. For a while there, before they finally pulled apart, Daniel wondered whether he and his new friend had become one person. Now they're definitely two people. From where we're standing, Hans is now slightly in shadow, facing one way, and Daniel has his back to us, facing the other.

This is the beginning of the end for them. After all, in a few days they will want to forget their mistakes here, and their all-night quest, and the best way to do that is silence. It'll be easy. They can swap numbers and email addresses, then not use them. But for now they hold themselves together, keep telling themselves they're doing something worthwhile. As we can see, Hans lights a cigarette, stops a local in the street and asks, *Can you recommend a bar where there will be absolutely no tourists?* A woman in her forties answers, *But if I tell you where it is, there will soon be two tourists there. Why don't you try the Tivoli? The queue seems to have gone down a little.* As the local woman walks away Hans says to Daniel, *She seemed cheerful. Maybe we should ask her for the secret.* But before they can act, she's gone, disappeared into the crowd. Hans suggests he and Daniel rest by the entrance a while. All this searching for happiness is exhausting.

If any of the above reminds you of your own life then simply step away. Nobody will blame you. Get back in the queue and have yourself a nice pleasant time — go up and down the rollercoaster, put off admitting the truth and get your picture taken with Pitzi, the Tivoli mascot.

I'll let you decide whether to stay here or leave; you are in charge of these adventures. If you're feeling wild you could leave the crowds and head out to Jutland to explore the area around Hald Sø and Dollerup Bakker (Hald Lake and the Dollerup Hills), or go to the stunning Mols Bjerge

National Park, right on the nose of Jutland, where you can witness first-hand the rolling hills formed at the end of the last ice age. Hire a bike: ride it. As you can see, cycling is popular here, and some of the cyclists are smiling. But it doesn't matter if you don't like physical exercise, there are many other ways to amuse yourself. Georg Carstensen (1812-1857) reminded King Christian VII (1786-1848) during his application for the original five year charter to create Tivoli, *When the people are amusing themselves, they do not think about politics.* But then, maybe some of us don't need to be distracted any more. The people of Denmark are happier than most. And you could be too, if you listen to the walls.

Alles, was ich mir Freude und die voraussichtlich [...]
überredete mich, verpflichten sich die Reise hatte mich
enttäuscht —. Sondern aus jenem Enttäuschung, ich habe eine
unerwartete Bildung erworben

THE MONOGAMY OPTICIAN

Lizzie's always saying we should go to one. Get our wandering eyes fixed.

Standing in the aisle at the front of the bus, the tour guide moves with the lurch and sway of the Booster 390, like she senses each movement in advance. Nothing surprises her. She's always smiling. She's wearing a cap that reads *URUGUAY* and a light blue national t-shirt with her name on the back. Lizzie leans in, whispering, *If Lucia's fifty, she looks pretty good for her age,* and I tell her for God's sake *SHUSH.* What I don't say is, why are human beings driven to seek out knowledge in the first place? Why can't we just accept our boundaries? And what's wrong with a little mystery? I can feel my mind unpacking, settling in for another marathon session of doubt.

Everything seems bigger than it is when we're on the road; I need to remember that before asking so many questions. But the back of this bus feels as hot as the sun's surface, the seats smell like burning tyres, the road underneath is a blistered volcano and one thing's for sure — I'll be up for hours tonight at the hostel window, mind like chocolate, thinking of a thousand other places I'd rather be while Lizzie sleeps as deep and as sound as if we were back at home, radiators humming. For Lizzie, the economy seats of the Booster 390 are a King Size in the Hilton. They're a health spa voucher, toe massage included. As for me, my mind is cooler when there's something simple to focus on. So I concentrate on Lucia, who is holding a football as a prop, explaining that *futbol is large part of Uruguayan culture.*

After the football, the Gaucho. Lucia gives us some background history (they're an ethnic group a bit like the United States cowboys or Ukrainian Cossacks, apparently), then she puts on a pretend Gaucho hat — *Given to me by my big strong Gaucho boyfriend!* She tips it to one side, smiles and explains that there is no more powerful symbol of freedom in this country than the Gaucho. She reminds us that the sky blue colour on the national flag is also a symbol for freedom, and says it's a while till our next stop, so we should relax and enjoy the scenery. *Not that our Argentinian cousins would admit it,* she declares, arms outstretched Jesus-like, gesturing to her nation's glory, *but Uruguay has most beautiful scenery in South America. Some scholars say, the world!* The scholars remain anonymous, and I don't have the *cojones* to ask for names.

Outside, the fields are becoming small houses, then fields again. *Look,* says Lizzie, warming me as she leans in, pointing out two cows that look like they're kissing. I laugh a while, then stop. I say to Lizzie, *That field is their home and they're having this intimate moment in what's basically their front room, while us two strangers spy on their sex life. We're peeping toms. If it was the other way round, we'd freak.* But when I get too serious Lizzie clams up so, in my lightest tone I add, *Do you think lesbian cows experience homophobic prejudice?* She laughs despite herself, and right then I want her on the floor of the Booster 390. I must give her the look or something cos she punches my arm and says, *Fucking hell, Samuel, we saved for, like, a hundred years. Stop with the filth and look at our planet will you?* I tell her, *When you sound like my mother, it only makes me want you more.*

Lizzie says she's not talking to me for the next five minutes. All mentions of my mother incur a standard penalty. The policy was agreed last Christmas and she can't understand why I won't keep to it.

Lucia makes a phone call and talks at speed. The words I can make out are *soledad, preocupado* and *Alfredo,* and as she talks, waving her hands, the speed and volume of Lucia's voice increases. The voice on the other end can't be saying much cos there are no breaks in her speech. Who is she talking to? Her husband? Son? Does Alfredo appreciate what she's doing here? This tour takes all day and she's already told us she runs it six times a week. Lucia looks like she could do with a year off, never mind a few days — perhaps I should suggest a home swap. You know, you live in my Wandsworth bedsit and I move into your seaside villa. Everyone wins!

After five minutes Lizzie taps my hand and says, *Hey, there's no point in this if you're not with me.* I make a face that shows I'm not playing that game, then, just to look anywhere but directly at her, I gaze up at the sky. It's a strange colour here. The blue behind these thick clouds seems to filter right through the whiteness, making them seem like luminous hot bulbs. Are clouds hot? They look like it from here, but then aren't they basically sponges in mid-air? And wouldn't that make them cold and wet? I don't have the patience for it, but for a moment I consider stopping everything, setting up camp right here on this bus and spending the rest of my life watching the sky.

Lucia cuts off her call without a goodbye then gestures towards a field of cows. Pointing at one she says, *This cow. Es muy importante para Uruguay!* Then she beams. She's been teaching us the phrase. Muttering it, feeling for sounds in my throat, I look up *cow* in the guide. It says there are way more cows than people in Uruguay. Here, the cow is queen. I say, *We should get a steak later. Essss mooyy imporrrrtaaaante para my stomach.* Lizzie slaps my leg, tells me to behave and I search her expression for whether she's joking. She is not joking. Seems to me the world is full of women who don't like their men very much, and men who don't know how to cope with that. A worldwide conspiracy prevents anyone from stating this publicly. It's the only explanation I can think of for why I haven't heard anyone say it out loud.

Lucia tells us *Uruguay* is a Guarani word meaning *river of shellfish* or *river the Uru birds come from.* I don't see how one word can mean both those things. I have no idea what an Uru is, though I can enjoy imagining what it looks like. (A bit like Big Bird from Sesame Street I reckon, only blue not yellow. And bilingual.) I don't know who the Guaranis are either, and if I'm honest, while Lucia talks and talks, all I can think of is what would happen if a band of Gauchos got on the bus, kidnapped Lizzie and took her away to their hideout. Would I cry? Dance on Sesame Street with the Uru birds? Would I shrug my shoulders and go speed dating? I look closely at Lizzie's face, those bright green eyes of hers and her rose-pink cheeks, and I think as hard as I can. I either love that face or I'm used to it. One of the two. After four years of looking at the same woman every morning, noon and night, how the hell are you supposed to tell the difference?

Somehow Lucia is back on football, saying Uruguay won the World Cup in both 1930 and 1950. The 1930 one was also hosted by Uruguay — 93,000 fans packed into the Estadio Centenario to see them defeat the *bastardos* of Argentina 4-2 in the final. Lucia talks like it happened last year and wasn't basically just them, Paraguay and the Faroe Islands playing for the World Cup in those days. Like most of Europe, Germany chose not to bother entering in 1930, and in 1950 they were banned. If you ask me, any World Cup without the Germans is void. But Lucia doesn't care. She holds up the football and grins, *Es muy importante para Uruguay.* Then it's onwards to the next roundabout. As we circle it she points at a tango festival advert and says, *Es muy importante para Uruguay.* Then she mentions Argentinian tango and snorts, a sour taste on her tongue. The middle-aged woman to our left whispers to her husband, *They think the tango's theirs you know,* and he grunts. I'm looking at her, mostly. Lizzie sees what I'm doing. *You think you know me,* I tell her, *but actually I'm an alien from the planet Uru and you know nothing of my ways.*

Lizzie says that's a ten minute penalty, and if I want to keep acting like an arsehole then she can keep this up all the way to São Paolo.

Lucia says the full name of this country is *República Oriental del Uruguay* and, unlike some nations such as the Bolivarian Republic of Venezuela — which shall remain nameless — here, we don't go changing the name of our homeland on the whim of Mr Small Penis Chavez who's obviously got a teeny tiny hard-on for Bolívar. Uruguayan independence was battled for against the oppressors of Buenos Aires, Rio and Madrid, and we take pride in our name, which derives from the fact that this land lies east of the Uruguay river, the most glorious branch of the Río de la Plata. She says the land mass of the country is about 68,000 square miles.

Lizzie says it's exhausting keeping up with who oppressed who, and that our book says it's *69,000* square miles.

Lucia says the population of Uruguay is 3.3 million, 1.8 million of whom live in Montevideo, a city originally set up as a military stronghold by the Spanish in the 18th Century. She says this country has triumphed over its colonial past and is now noted in South America for low levels of corruption and good working conditions. Also for handsome men and pretty ladies. The government provides every schoolchild with a laptop and free internet. Uruguay was one of only two South American countries which did not go into recession in the late 2000s because we know how to handle money and don't go gifting it to bankers.

Lizzie wonders aloud how anyone can be a thousand *anythings* out in their calculations, doubts Lucia understands the collapse of the banking system and says, *What else might she have got wrong? Why are we listening to all these figures, and how do we know we can trust them?*

I say that, in the grand scheme of things, a thousand isn't such a big number. Also, all small nations advertise themselves to foreigners by emphasising the good parts of their history and filing away the bad, doesn't she know that by now? I remind her she's not supposed to be talking to me, and that's hardly the way to prove she can keep this up till São Paolo.

Lucia says the climate is generally mild. It's never freezing here. Perhaps some of you Brits should consider emigrating, no? Then your children can get free laptops.

Lizzie says there are ten million people in São Paolo, and when she gets there she's gonna go onto getmeabig gaucho.com, get herself a big Gaucho who knows how to treat a woman, and I won't last five minutes without her.

I agree she's probably right, I would struggle to cope without her, but point out that

a. the Gauchos are different in Brazil, they're called Vaquieros, and they're only found in the North,
b. Gauchos aren't around anymore anyway, and
c. I'm afraid she's still talking to me.

Lizzie says I always have to have the last word.

I tell her yes I do. Because her last one is usually wrong. Lucia says, *KEEP IT DOWN AT THE BACK PLEASE,* and that by the nineteenth century the indigenous population had sadly been wiped out here. Now if you see someone that looks like an African in Uruguay then that means their people were slaves brought over to work in the ports in the processing of meat. Either that or they're one of those rich black tourists you sometimes get these days.

Lizzie says Lucia is a racist and she wants to get off the bus. That thing about the meat is disgusting.

I raise my hands but before I can say anything she tells me to go fuck myself.

Lucia says that if you think they speak Spanish like the Spaniards in this country then you don't know very much now do you?

I tell Lizzie we're not getting off the bus and ask why she can't ever just enjoy herself? (I don't wait for an answer.) She doesn't deserve to see the majesty of the great nation of the Uru birds. She chose this tour cos she wanted to cram in Chile, Peru and Paraguay as well as Argentina and Brazil, that she'd insisted on it cos we were only in Uruguay a few days and it was *good to have someone to show us the important stuff.* I don't know why I agreed. Our whole route was made in a park in Europe, she picked these countries cos she liked the names, neither of us thought through the logistics of zig-zagging the entire vast continent of South America and now I can't think of a single reason to see the plan through. Lizzie starts crying, buries her head in my shoulder and whispers that she misses her mum. She says sorry, kisses me softly on the lips and asks me not to leave her. Now she's laughing and crying at the same time. I wipe away her tears with my finger, say sorry too, and tell her I wouldn't want to be anywhere else.

This is the way things are.

The other young couple on this trip are two seats ahead of us, taking photographs and notes like this is a school trip. We hold hands and Lizzie leans on me, watching them. I bring her left hand up to my shoulder and peck it as I'm looking at the sky, avoiding looking at the other couple who are either much happier than us or just don't argue in public. I think about saying, *I love you even when I hate you,* but I've promised to keep that kind of bullshit to a minimum after arguments. We're just having an ordinary row about not very much. Couples do that all the time. This is only a tour, it's nothing special. Anyone can come to Uruguay, book online, see a cow and fancy a steak. It's hardly Columbus territory — and as Lizzie would say, Columbus had *some serious bullshit issues* of his own. Up the front of the bus, Lucia's talking about colonisation, the independence struggle and the true spirit of the Uruguayan people, as the Booster 390 pulls a hard right. Then she's talking the tango again. That woman has three areas of expertise — *futbol,* the tango and the *bastardos* of Argentina — and she's swapping between them at will.

You want to go to a show tonight? I ask Lizzie. *I don't care really, as long as we're together. Hey, what do you think an Uru bird looks like?* Lizzie sits up, leans away, doesn't answer. Sometimes she thinks it's unnecessary.

I think about going home twenty or thirty times a day.

At home, I thought about escaping twenty or thirty times a day.

I bought a travel diary then left it in a Caffè Nero at Heathrow. Now so much is happening and I don't have paper with me. As soon as it's over I'll forget how it made me feel and in twenty years I'll wonder why I'm still making the same mistakes.

When we pass the sign saying *WELCOME TO MONTEVIDEO*, there's a round of applause like this is a flight in a hurricane and Lucia is a pilot who's ensured a smooth landing smack bang on the centre of the strip. She gestures to the elderly man on her left, begins to clap and says, *Julio the driver, everybody!* Julio gets applause too, which he acknowledges with a slow nod of the head. We can see the sea from here. It's shiny and aqua blue. Heat seems to be rising from its surface. It looks nothing like any sea I've witnessed before and for a moment I think to myself, maybe I've underestimated it here.

Every thought I have erases the one before.

I don't know how travellers are supposed to feel, but I don't think it's kicked in for me yet. Maybe cos we've only been going a few months — or cos we never thought of something to do. Then we'd have stories — *Oh man, let me tell you about this slave driver we worked for out in the 'Guay — Oh man, the crazy people out there* — but as it is, all we've done is buy overpriced coffees in near-identical squares, argued and obsessed over whether the camera is in the bag. (I reach for it. The camera hasn't moved.) The bus bumps and squeaks, the engine splutters and I've been in motion for years. But I don't have to be, right? Strapping young white men like me are in charge of this planet. At the next village I can flatten a barn door and impregnate the nearest farm girl — she'll notice a prize bull waltzing into her kitchen, down my skinny jeans, pull me right into

her and cry out, *Dear God, give me children!* As we press on
into strange countries it's good to know that for people like
us, life is full of options.

I said that this morning. Lizzie was choosing a dress
and I was waiting for her to get on with it. She asked me
to pick one of two, I shrugged my shoulders and said, *Life
is full of options.* (Which I now recognise was not the right
thing to do.) She played with her pony tail and answered,
Yeah, too many, but without even looking at me, and in that
voice that basically means: can you believe we were born
in this century? Now what that means is: Lizzie thinks the
whole world is waving our way, giving us the V's, daring
us to make the best of it or else admit we're not fit to share
surnames with our ancestors who could probably:

1. kill tigers with their bare hands,
2. sew buttons on dresses without taking forever to get
   it right and having a crying fit halfway through,
3. find their way out of the woods in the dark, and
4. didn't even have Google Maps.

This takes some untangling, but what my beloved partner
means by THAT bunch of crap is: she's absolutely 100%
sure there's a single man out there who's got a thing for
29-year-old dirty blondes with small breasts, who can
navigate the bus system of South America, who earns
twice my salary, has a thicker, longer cock than mine
and a better idea of how to use it. Every night she stays
is a temporary commitment and she's prepared to go no
further.

Lizzie knows the above information cos even out here
she has round the clock internet access on her phone and
iPad which show her relevant examples of the form. Even
before she's done typing the words, the search engine

knows what she's looking for.

Some dude in Kennington called Charles claims he's got the full set and has offered to send pictures.

For the same reason Lizzie knows these things, I know these things. At nights, I search her History while she sleeps. I know her passwords. And even if I wasn't tracking her every email, I know that these days there are no Reachers and Settlers any more. We're basically all Settlers, knowing there's an improved model out there on the market if only we could be bothered to chase it down. This means the longest living generation in history will make precious few Diamond wedding anniversary speeches. Being Settlers makes our eyes run out of our heads, and if there really was such a thing as a Monogamy Optician then some smart arse would make a killing, taking our money then training our gazes on each other like sparrows in neck braces who can't quite make out the cancan dancers high-kicking at the edges of our vision. It's bullshit of course but Lizzie's forever saying the internet was the start of modern infidelity. As it happens, it was the last thing she said as we climbed on the Booster 390 this morning. I was polite, quiet, I'm not looking to humiliate anyone. But I did say, as I was putting our rucksacks into the hold, *I respect what you're saying, darling, but in another way, the start was when you began fucking Hardeep from the office.*

That was a fifteen minute penalty. We've agreed to put that behind us.

I've no idea how long I've been away in my mind, or if I've said anything out loud.

Lizzie is dozing next to me, head resting on the shaking window. All windows shake on the buses out here. I don't know what they're so nervous about.

To stop myself thinking, I fix my gaze on an elderly man who's rolling slowly down the dirt path we're cutting through, a wild dog panting at his feet. Most people here have never left this country and look like they couldn't care less. Don't they know how many countries there are out there? Don't they feel like they should go and check a few out? I'm so jealous I could spit. I'm so tense I could rip myself apart. Like I tell Lizzie some nights, in these hostels, when we're laying down to sleep and holding each other (but not making love) — if sometimes it seems like I'm acting overwhelmed, it's because actually, *I feel overwhelmed.*

The bus chugs on. Lucia is slumped in her chair by the driver as if she's exhausted herself with all that enthusiasm for her country, while Lizzie wakes and leans over, reaching for the guide as you might reach for a glass of water during the night. It helps her, thinking she knows what's coming, and without the guide she wouldn't be able to sit still — so I say nothing. Relationships are all compromise. If you're looking for a partner who's got no quirks or weaknesses or backstory, who's all you've ever dreamed of, then dreamland's the only place you're gonna find them, right? But is there anyone out there like me who thinks it's fun to take the wrong turn and maybe end up in a ditch or a police station? If there is, I'd like to be introduced. I've got no idea how me and Lizzie are still together. Yesterday's a faint memory. The night we hooked up is a story we've told so many times, the truth has little to do with it. The woman two seats in front seems like she might be my kind of girl. Her legs stretch over her boyfriend. She's not wearing any sandals and not looking at him like he's a piece of shit.

I wish something would happen, I say to Lizzie.

Something is happening, she replies, flicking through the book. *Just not fast enough for you.*

Lucia tells us to get comfortable, there's nothing to see here.

I've only known her a couple of hours but that doesn't sound like the Lucia I've grown to love. I think about going up to the front and asking if she's okay. Asking her out on a date. Putting an arm around her possibly-fifty-year-old shoulders, giving them a nice slow massage, asking who Alfredo is and also, does she ever wonder if she picked the wrong guy? I wouldn't mind telling Lucia as I knead my fingers into her back: Lizzie thinks about that every day, and my wandering eyes are getting worse. Lizzie leans her head back on my shoulder, still damp from her tears, and begins circling places to stay, making notes about safety issues to consider. She puts her thumb in her mouth and begins to suck. What I want to say is, *This isn't safety.*

Lizzie's head drifts into my lap as she's reading and writing. I imagine closing her eyes, putting her back to sleep and asking Lucia if Julio will let me off the bus right here. I could wander back to the fields and hang out with the cows for a few days. Wander back to the bus stop again. Wait until a bus comes by to take me to The Monogamy Optician. I'd wait for the doors to open and ask the driver, *Do you believe in lifelong love affairs? Is everyone else on the bus going to have their eyes fixed?* Maybe it's not our fault that all we can think about is the people we could be sleeping with, if only we weren't sleeping with each other. Maybe the guilt is a waste of time. What I can't admit out loud is, since the sex stopped a year ago, I have loved Lizzie like a sister, and not very much like a lover. I think about kissing her forehead before I go, leaving her a note that says, *Safe journey home.* As if this was all part of the plan.

Our bus pulls up outside a small market which, it occurs to me, may be there because we are. There are toilets here. There's one café. Lucia springs back to life and shouts

MATÉ BREAK as she leaps off the bus. We're getting off in her wake and she leads us towards four men standing in front of rugs covered with trinkets. They're cradling cups of hot herby maté in the heat like this is Reykjavik, not Montevideo, and they're falling about joking — what they're doing isn't even work. It's just part of life, which is a bit of a laugh and nothing more. I could climb into the skin of one of these men and hide. I could stay there for years and no one would even know. All four men wolf whistle at Lucia and in an instant her walk becomes a bounce. I realise that if I had the chance, and I knew Lizzie wouldn't find out, I would definitely fuck this woman who is bouncing along towards her dedicated maté-selling fans. I think about saying to Lizzie, *I love you but you can't trust me. Listen to this thought I just had! It's sick!*

Lucia claps her hands to hurry us troops, then puts her arms round a couple of the men and says, *Buy buy buy! Great traditional gifts for your wife. Your girlfriend. Maybe you want to buy something for both wife AND girlfriend!* Then she laughs like the idea of anyone having a single partner is ridiculous. I wonder which of this bunch is her bit on the side — and if one of them is Alfredo. She brings out a hand mirror, whips it open, checks her make-up and closes it again, satisfied, while around her the members of our group fight for a viewing spot, their wallets already out. The maté cups on the rug below are all being snapped up. Lucia points at them and says, *Everybody! New good maté, real authentic Uruguayan — Eeeeeessss?* The middle-aged man from the bus interrupts her just in time, answering: *Muy importante para Uruguay!* His wife tells him to have some respect but Lucia won't have her spoiling everyone's fun. *No no no no, he's right,* she says. *Es MUY importante para Uruguay.*

As we follow Lucia, who's telling us the history of this drink and why it's so *importante* for her people who lived unjustly blah blah for so long in the shadow of a larger, not-so-great blah de blah, I realise the two of us are just one small, easily forgotten part of this group. Down a side street, two of the maté guys are now in conversation, and I wonder what life lives down there. How you get to it. Behind them, the view: the narrow street goes on into the distance, over a hill, then dips deliciously out of sight. I look at Lizzie. We could be gone. I could be gone — into the hills, the fields — and no one would even know I went on purpose. Maybe they'd think I'd been kidnapped by a Gaucho. Lizzie could mourn and feel fine about it. I could go in search of the mysterious Uru bird. I find myself wanting to run down the side street, leaving my rucksack behind, flapping my wings till I take off. Then I remember that, on the road, everything seems bigger to me than it actually is, and the feeling passes. I had my chance and let it go. People spend whole lives like this.

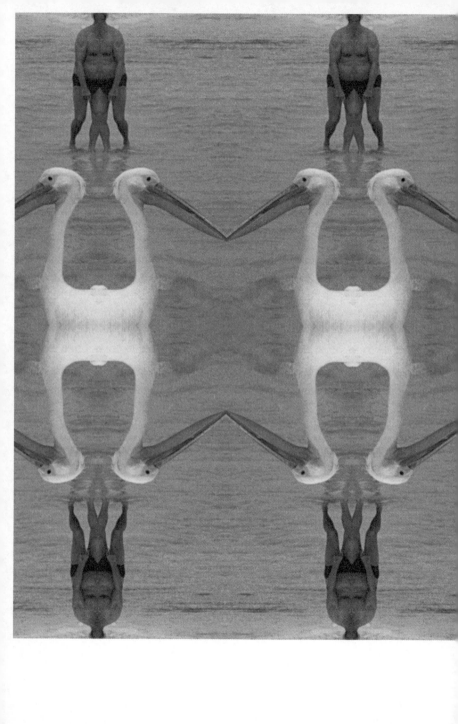

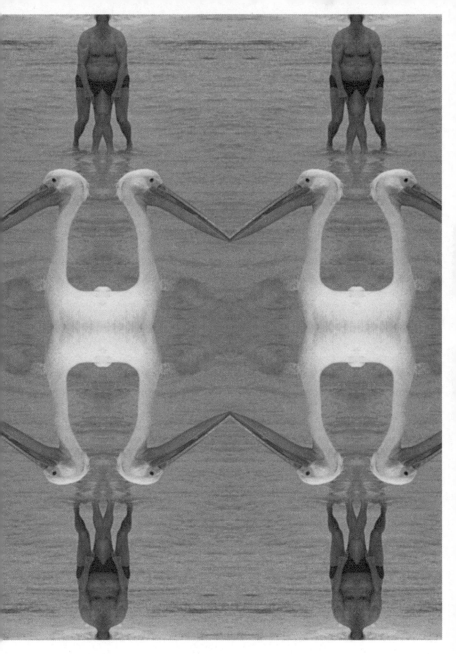

Mae popeth yr wyf yn disgwyl i roi i mi lawenydd ac sy'n
[...] fy mherswadio i ymgymryd â'r daith wedi fy siomi —.
Ond allan o'r siom iawn, yr wyf wedi cael gafael ar addysg
annisgwyl

AFTER DRINK YOU CAN TURN EARTH UP SIDE DOWN

In this club in downtown Hong Kong the waitresses never let your glass get below midway before offering you another drink. They all look eighteen or nineteen. They all look good. They're wearing tartan skirts above the knee and ties pulled loose over part-open white shirts, like someone's got halfway to undressing them before deciding against it. The emblems on the waitresses' shirts read: *WAN CHAI AMAZON: A WHOLE NEW ADVENTURE!* As four or five of them zip between tables, talking in hand signals to punters *(You want another beer or not?)*, I think to myself: we're probably the youngest men in here. Then I think: it was funny, the way Angie put it. *Our baby is born. Come and see.* Like I was expecting the news and understood. Like it's not a twenty thousand mile round trip from England to visit. Looking down, I notice my bag is poking out from underneath my stool, the panda toy and fake road sign I got at the market spilling out onto the floor. I don't bend down. With one swift kick I push them both back in the bag, the contents resting under a nearby table. Then I shout into Nick's ear. *Lot of westerners in here,* I say.

Nick doesn't reply straight away. He's watching the dance floor, where the first few brave souls of the night are trying out their moves to Eric Clapton's 'Cocaine'. Three couples are having a good time. One especially. A young local girl is slow-swaying along to the live band with a white guy in an Armani suit. Maybe he's sixty, or older. The girl laughs at something the man says, claps her hand onto his chest then lets it run down the buttons of his shirt — one button, two buttons, three — before her slim fingers rest on his belly, lingering just above his belt. Her nails stroke him ever so slightly, slow and soft. The guy grins. Life's just too fucking good, isn't it? When he sees me looking, he winks, like I'm next in line or something. I give him the finger but he's not even surprised. He answers by licking his lips and whipping the girl round, fast, in a circle. Nick grabs more monkey nuts from the bowl, drops the shells on the floor and faces me. *Yeah, yeah,* he says, readjusting his baseball cap. *So what?*

I've forgotten the question I asked, or if I asked a question at all. *So nothing,* I say, keeping my voice light, one palm on his shoulder as I lean in to be heard. *Hey, you were right. Fucking GREAT band here. I mean. Just — fucking — GREAT.* These last few days, I lie without thinking. I talk without noticing. Sometimes, I don't know where I am. I wake up during the night, stagger to the hotel room toilet and think I'm already there, in my new home in the sun, Angie sleeping and the baby in the cot by our bed. Angie stirs and says, *Sweetie, come back.* But here, now, I say to Nick, *This place is a real find.* And it sounds like I mean it.

After a few songs I sneak a look at the score. No change. So I turn back. It's probably rude to check the football while these guys are ripping into 'Wish You Were Here' as if they wrote it themselves, as if they're really trying to

tell us something. But then, it's not like we're watching
the real thing. In some shitty bar next to a strip club. On
a Tuesday night in April. And besides, everyone seems to
be doing it. Just before they go for one last chorus I even
catch the keyboard player, this guy who looks like a tribal
Indian or something, craning for a view from his place
at the back of the stage. But no luck: the stocky, Zen-like
bass man is in his way. One of the two guitar players is to
his left, knees bent, chin to the heavens, riffing in front of
the other screen. The drummer, complete with full classic
rock uniform — ponytail, hair dyed black to cover the
grey, skull tattoos, faded Sabbath t-shirt — is crammed at
the back, his cymbals in that bit too close to him, blocking
the smallest screen. That's the one by the exit. Or the toilet.
Or both. There are no signs on anything around here. Up
front, the singer and other guitar player hover at the edge
of the stage — in their minds, this is a different crowd.
One's doing the lead vocal, the other the harmony. Both
have their eyes closed. *Oh, how I wish you were here,* they
sing, crouching for effect. Then standing straight. Then
opening their eyes again. The two of them, in unison. Like
this outpouring of emotion, it's sudden, unexpected.

Just as I'm thinking of jumping up there and joining
them, dipping and stretching in symmetry, letting the
sounds conquer me too, a tartan skirt comes by, picking
up two empties and looking around for more. I don't
wait for a hand signal. I give a couple of my own, waving
her over, then pointing to our three-quarter full bottles.
She smiles, all cheeky, like I've just done something
witty or interesting and I think, *I could get used to it here.*
Meanwhile, Nick's far away. He's been singing along,
his whole body consumed, feeling the thumps and chord
changes along with the band as he lunges back and
forth on his stool, playing the drums on his knees, his

gym-toned muscles taut and visible through a t-shirt probably chosen cos it's ever so slightly too small. I wonder if Nick's high. I met him three hours ago. How the hell would I know what Nick's like high? Or sober? Or sad? It feels like an age before 'Wish You Were Here' finally finishes, the ripple of applause and whoops slowly dies down, and he starts talking again. Like we never stopped. Like, in this place, time doesn't pass unless Nick says so. *These guys play here every night,* he tells me. *Ten till six thirty in the morning. Three full sets. Can you believe that? They know, like, six hundred songs, man. You name it. You fucking name it. They know it. The Stones. The Beatles. Anything.* Trying to keep my face straight, I say, *They do any African stuff? I like African music.* Nick comes in closer, checks to see if I'm just passing the time, then backs away. *Probably,* he says, finally. *What's wrong? You don't like The Rolling Stones?* We've not paid for the drinks yet. I decide to play nice. *Every night they play?* I say. *Wow.* Nick nods. Relaxes. Smiles. *Yeah. Well. They get two nights off a month.* I answer, *Must need a lot of stamina. And strong wrists!* I laugh dirty. Let him work it out.

Another few seconds pass before I take a good long swig on my drink, which is actually, no shit, called *Hong Kong Beer.* There aren't even any Chinese characters on the side of the bottle. I think, *this fucking place!* Then I think of how far I am from Australia, and how long it takes to get there. Then how long it takes to get from the airport to the city. From the city to Angie's. From her front door to the back room, where my boy could be sleeping, right now. I try and imagine his little nose. His ears. His smell. I wonder what name she gave him and why she didn't tell me on the phone. A wave of heat passes through me as I allow myself to hope she named him after me. I shake my head, forget where I am, then it comes back.

These boys make a lot of money? I ask Nick, pointing to the band with my bottle. This place is filling up. Nick laughs, snorts. *You've not been here long, have you my friend?* Nick can fuck right off if he thinks I'm rising to that. I'm not even supposed to be here. *Back soon,* I tell him, keeping it cheerful. *Going for a cancer stick.*

Standing up, I notice the back of my jeans are soaking wet. Behind me, an old man in Bermuda shirt and shorts who can't be much less than seventy is having a good time, laughing at the cocktail glass he's just knocked over me like he's fascinated by it, like he's never seen a spilt drink before. The teenagers either side of him are laughing too. So hard it sounds like anger. The old man says, *Sorry dude,* laughs some more and says, *Lemme buy you another one,* but shows no signs of actually getting up, doing it, or helping me dry off. I forget what I got up for in the first place.

As I clean myself up in the toilet I think: it feels like a long time since I stood at that airport gate, boarding pass in hand, watching my connection get smaller and smaller and disappear into a paper cut in the sky. For a while, I forgot about the cost — I was just looking at that paper cut, a narrow slit that let a plane through into the other side of the world, my maybe future: Angie, responsibility, the end of late nights and stupid mistakes. Back in the club, I rub my jeans with a paper towel. It's not helping. I remember watching that plane leaving and thinking, *I could just hide.* That was a week ago. Today's the third straight morning I've got up late, hungover to hell, sat with a strong coffee in Starbucks in Tsim Sha Tsui and stared into my coffee cup imagining the bubble in my drink is a plane, or a ship, making its way across the water. Wondering what I'm waiting for. I don't know where the days have gone. This morning, Angie's message read: *You coming or not?*

When I get back from the toilet Nick's joking with the band, between numbers, maybe making a request. I look down and see that in among the monkey shells and the stickiness of spilt drinks, my bag has moved again. Or disappeared. Looking around on the floor, under tables, behind chairs, stumbling around blindly, I know I'm not going to see it. I remember buying the sign this morning: above a series of Chinese characters that could have meant just about anything it said *AFTER DRINK YOU CAN TURN EARTH UP SIDE DOWN.* A few hours ago, that made me laugh. I can't remember why. It was supposed to be a translation of something, maybe a proverb. Something wise in a Chinese dialect made silly by the English language. What did I buy the sign for? And what about the panda?

The band are doing 'Hotel California' now, the two guitarists smiling as they faithfully play out the instrumental note for note as a duo, in harmony. It sounds like the oldest song in the world. Tired, almost dead. A dead song from a long-dead age. But these boys are trying their best to bring it back to life. They look like there's nothing else in the world they'd rather be doing than playing the instrumental from 'Hotel California'. The whole scene gives me a shiver. You can feel something spilling out of them, these musicians, into the room and round the whole place, the whole street, all over the Wan Chai district, throughout Hong Kong. And Nick's right with it, fist pumping in the air. When the song finishes, there's damn near a standing ovation. The singer takes off his hat, bows low and says, *Hong Kong — you are too kind!*

Hey, Nick, these guys local? I ask. *Filipino, dude. You know nothing?* I shrug. Nick shakes his head. *They left the Philippines together — all still live together too, in an apartment near here. And they still send most of their money home. Good boys. Fucking tragedy it is. Fucking triumph.*

I say, *Right. What?* I'm trying to concentrate on Nick's eyes, though they're spinning now. *They went to Japan first. The Japanese are good musicians, you know, but fuck it, the truth is, their language can't cope with English sounds. Wrong shaped mouths. Good news for Filipinos! So they worked in Japan. Then here.* Nick rubs his index finger and thumb together. *More green,* he says. *But still slavery.* It feels like my turn to speak. To say wow again, or give an opinion.

Though I'm thinking of something else, somewhere else, I ask, *Do they play their own stuff?* He says, *They could do that. Their songs are amazing. The best songs on this planet if you ask me. But what are you gonna do?* He waves a hand dismissively at the crowd. I think to myself, yeah. Nick's definitely high. *That's a shame,* I tell his spinning eyes. *Really.* The band, I notice, is spinning too. Bass drum, spinning. Guitars, spinning. Dancers, screens, stools. All moving, in beautiful circles. Then more drinks land on our table and more empties are taken away. I don't remember drinking them. *I dig it though,* says Nick. *A lot of guys here are a long way from home. They want something that reminds them of what they're missing.*

I say, *Then why don't they stay there then? I mean, they're just here for money, right? And to get laid?* Nick puts his drink down hard on the table. The froth surges up the neck, over the lip of the bottle and down the sides of the label reading *Hong Kong Beer. Look, buddy.* He searches his brain for my name. Draws a blank. *You know fuck all about this place, alright?* Nick clocks me checking out one of the tartan skirts zipping by. *You come in here, spit on us and leave.* He says, whispering the final word, *You types make me sick.*

I don't know what that means but I do know his eyebrows have become one bushy line that won't sit still. Why not? Why won't it sit still? His pupils are spirals.

I laugh.

Nick says, *Insult my people again and I'll kill you.*

His face is hard now, the whole thing, like it's set in concrete.

Your people? I say. *I thought you were from West Virginia.*

I look around the club, thinking, *I could stay here forever.* Thinking, *I've got to get out of here.* Thinking, *but where to?* For a second it looks like Nick's going to boil over, frothing at the mouth, just like his beer. Like he's going to hit me. But he just downs his drink, grabs his coat and leaves. Then, as if he's planned it, the skirt comes by with the bill. Just a skirt. No smile. No woman inside. I pay and move to a barstool to watch the rest of the show.

I don't sit on my own for long. As the band kick into 'Crosstown Traffic' I feel an arm slip through mine, and a hand fall on the small of my back.

Hello, says a voice.

Hello, I say back. Then, *My son is born. I'm not supposed to be here.*

That nice, says the voice, who also has a warm body, which has already pulled in close. Guitar Man Number 1 is changing over his instrument to one which is pretty battered, with black stains around the sides. I reckon I know what's coming. This is Hendrix, after all. The suits expect.

I not supposed to be here too, says the voice.

Then what are you doing here? I ask.

I come to Hong Kong to make business, says the voice and body with hands. And after a moment, *Monkey business!*

Then a grin, a giggle. She smells like perfume, like sweat.

I have a family, I say. *I'm going to see them.*

Good. Our secret then. Monkey business?

It's not funny, so I don't know why I smile. Laugh again. Can't stop.

No way, I say, still laughing. *No more trouble.*

That's why they went to...

England, yes? I go to England. We get married. I have lots of sons.

I finish the drink in front of me in one gulp, though I don't know if it's mine.

No. Not England. You know what... Fuck it. Sorry. I can't.

It's hard to get words out now.

The voice and body is a girl, who looks young but old too. Her eyes say, *I know you.* Her lips say, *I know you.* Her hands say, *I know you.* She pouts, fake sad, pulling one of those little girl faces that must work on the guys out here. Seconds pass. Nothing happens.

Then the pout is gone and she says, *If you can't then what you doing here?*

Her voice is clipped. The night is short.

Hey. You hear me? What you doing here?

When I don't answer, she follows my gaze. The guy in the Armani suit is down the front now, the dance floor is full, and he's bowing down in tribute as Guitar Player Number 1 sets his instrument alight for the first time tonight. Then the guy stands, lets out a yell, looks around, and sees me again. Just for a moment. And he smiles. In his eyes, it's 1970. He's young, single, before divorce and kids and decades in sales, before escaping East to forget. Here, when he walks down the street, everyone wants to say *hi*. When he talks, people listen. Life's just too fucking good, isn't it? He raises his beer to the skies, mimes along to 'Crosstown Traffic' and pulls his new girl towards him for one more kiss.

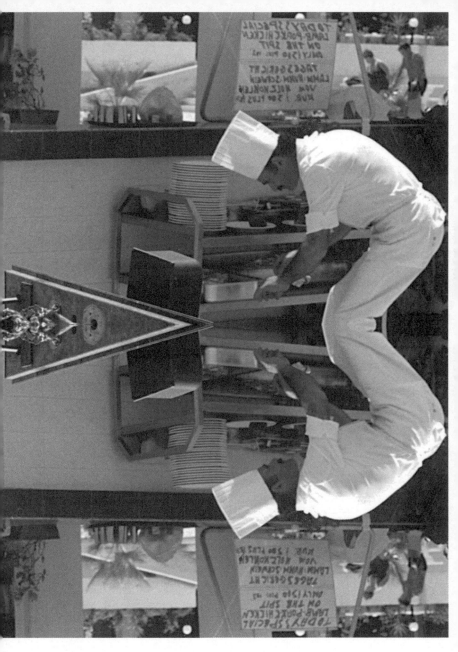

Tutto ciò che mi aspettavo di darmi piacere e che [...] mi ha convinto a intraprendere il viaggio mi aveva deluso —., Ma su che delusione molto, ho acquisito una formazione inaspettata

I KNOW MY TEAM AND I SHALL NOT BE MOVED

He was in the downstairs lounge again. As I parked the car, I could just about make him out through the front window — thinner now but still distinctive, even from a distance. Shoulders hunched. Back bent. Wiry frame. He was sitting with four or five others, dwarfed by one of those high-backed pink seats that reach halfway to the ceiling. Probably bought on the cheap years ago, in bulk. You shouldn't skimp on chairs. Especially in a place like that where you have to sit in them all day, looking at other people sitting in them all day. I turned off the engine and sat in the dark, hands tight around the wheel, just watching: my father was leaning forward, talking intently to the man next to him. Then he smiled. I made myself get out of the car, locked it and approached the buzzer, giving my name and the reason for my visit.

The automatic doors parted slowly and I walked through, trying to be confident, act relaxed, as if I came to see him every day or every week, not once or twice a year. As if I'd been there all morning and just popped out to do an errand, maybe stopping on the way back to buy something for his sweet tooth that I just knew would make his day. The doors whirred shut behind me and the strong smell of antiseptic hit hard. I'd forgotten about that. Also, how the layout of the lounge reminded me of a school corridor. A week-to-week timetable of events and day trips was written in large print, attached to a notice board on one wall, next to a Hebrew calendar peppered with festival dates and posters advertising future group activities. Today was Shabbat, so that explained the decorations.

Hi, Dad, I said, leaning over to give him a kiss. *Shall we have a drink?*

Oh, there you are… Thanks but I don't drink any more… I used to be an alcoholic you know.

I was thinking of something hot.

Tea then. Milk, no sugar. Sweet enough already.

I'd never heard his voice so soft or broken. He had to keep pausing for breath and he looked pale, gaunt. David had warned me, last week, when he phoned from his surgery. He told me to be prepared. He said I was going to be shocked. I said he was obviously just trying to upset me and put the phone down.

I'll see to it in a minute, I replied, forcing a smile. *Shall we sit over here?*

I gestured to a nearby empty table, which faced out onto the pretty, perfectly ordered gardens by the road. My father eyed the table carefully, considered whether there was any reason he should avoid this step into the unknown, then nodded in reluctant agreement, pulling me near so I could help him up.

My daughter, he said to the circle, wobbling slightly as he rose, swaying between the walking stick on his left side and me on his right. *Good girl… Most of the time.*

The circle gave a murmur of weak approval. One of them was asleep, and at least one other was slumped in her chair, half awake.

What do you do? said one man. *Are you the doctor?*

That's my brother, I replied. *I... Well... I haven't done much recently. But that's all about to change.*

A different man, who might have been asleep when I arrived, sat up and said, *I know which one you are. Married yet?*

No. Still happily unmarried, thank you.

Another murmur started up.

Don't blame me for that, said Dad, his voice rising in anger, gathering in strength. *I did my best. The world is full of wonder, I told her. Get out there! Live! Love! Dance! Roll around in the grass!* He shook his head slowly. *But look at her. Forty-two and still lost. No job, no man, no fucking future. Her mother, God rest her soul, she was so ashamed.*

Don't swear, Albert, said the other man, nodding in the direction of a sleeping woman to his left. *There are ladies present.*

Dad ignored him and turned to me, looking hard now. Gripping my forearm tight with his bony hand. It was so thin, it was more like a vulture's claw.

I do love you, though, he said, tired again, having exhausted himself with his last speech. *You big fat bugger. I don't know why, but I love you. Let Hashem strike me down dead if I don't...*

Well, nice to meet you all, I said to the circle, directing Dad towards the other table as fast as I could. I helped him into his new seat, just yards from the old one, then sat down next to him.

Come here. Come closer, he whispered. *I want to tell you something.*

I leaned in and he jabbed a finger towards one of the men who'd been talking to us. *That's Bert Silverman. A real alter cocker, that one.*

Be nice, Dad. He's your cousin.

Your cousin. On your mother's side. After she died I thought I'd never have to see him again. Such a khazer he was when the business was falling apart. He owed me a thousand pounds. That was a lot of money in those days! And did I get an apology? You must be joking! They say he left his wife for some shikseh. Moved to Birmingham. Or was it Manchester?

This is Manchester, Dad… right here. This is where you grew up. See that street opposite? I pointed out of the window. *We lived on the other side of that street. By the park.*

He carried on thinking aloud.

They always come back home to die. You noticed that? Half the kids at my fucking Bar Mitzvah are in this place. He waved a weak hand in the direction of the others. *Not that any of us chose it. Thrown in together. Emptied out into this stinking dustbin full of miserable faces by the children we raised. I survived the Holocaust, you know. I used to be strong. But look at me now. My children shit on me.* He looked up, remembering who he was talking to. *No offence. You understand.*

I thought you liked Bert Silverman, I answered, clasping my hands tight between my legs. *Remember, I told you he was here? You were pleased. We talked about it. We chose this place because we thought you'd have friends.*

Dad folded his arms. *And enemies.*

I smiled and stood up. *I'll get the tea now. Back soon.*

As I walked away, I couldn't help but feel proud. I didn't even tell him off for swearing. I was going to be fine. And this wasn't going to go on for much longer.

I ran into the Sister in the corridor. I smiled and went to move past her but she ushered me into her office, closed the door and asked me to sit me down. She spoke in a kind, steady voice about what she called *your father's case.*

While I sat there, trying not to listen, she talked about

why she believed people chose Lieberman Homes for their loved ones, what the homes offered, how elderly people often liked things they knew well, how they were most comfortable in their own communities, and how that was fine. How maybe it was difficult for some people to understand, but those different generations saw the world in a different way and that really that was OK, wasn't it? We might think they're silly, but we should try to understand, shouldn't we? Especially after what my father had been through. One day, she said, our children would probably laugh at our stuffy old opinions. They way we dress. How we behave. That was something to look forward to, wasn't it? She laughed but I didn't know why. She was asking too many questions. Her voice was a faraway noise. Her hands were steady, nails painted, immaculate. All I could think of was what I was going to say to Dad, and how I didn't trust myself to get the drinks to the table without spilling hot liquid all over my hands.

Would you carry them please? I said.

I'm sorry?

I mean, would you carry the drinks to the table for us?

The Sister didn't understand. *You don't have any drinks,* she said.

Two teas. Milk, no sugar. Sweet enough already. That's what I'm here for. I'd really appreciate it because my hands shake and... and... and I can't help it.

My voice faded to nothing. The Sister put her hand gently over mine.

Do you understand? Your father's condition has deteriorated greatly since you were last here. He had another fall two days ago. Now, I know you find this difficult, but you really must try not to repeat the kind of incidents we've had with your previous visits. Please try to make allowances, for your father's sake. Be patient with him. Don't take anything he says too seriously.

He does have occasional lucid moments, but mostly he doesn't know what he's doing or saying any more. Grumpiness is a side effect of the condition — any of us would be the same. Speak to your brother about this. He's here most days. He knows.

She removed her hand from mine and smiled, back to her standard professional voice — cheerful, understanding, but firm too. *We have a great deal of experience in this kind of thing and, I assure you, the best we can do is make him as comfortable as possible. There are a few simple rules that will help. Do you think you can remember them?*

Yes, I said, straightening my skirt, then looking at the floor. Then out of the window. Then back down at the floor again.

The first and most important rule is to never correct him. If he says it's 1974, it's 1974. OK? Sometimes he's happier in the past, or in another country — though any talk of war upsets him, naturally. He still gets occasional flashbacks. Also, if he repeats something, don't tell him he's said it before. If he's forgotten something, don't remind him. You wouldn't know it from how he is today, naughty thing, but your father is actually perfectly content much of the time. He enjoys celebrating the festivals and retains a strong religious belief, which is usually good for the health of patients in this situation. He's kind to others. He can be very good socially. But he's only happy when he forgets that the world he lives in is his own. If he's reminded of his condition, or made to feel foolish, then he's likely to get confused. And perhaps aggressive. Right?

Yes.

The second thing is, try not to show him you're distressed. He will sense the reason for this, and he'll react. Remember — this is not his fault.

I see.

And thirdly, try not to give him any demanding news. Well-meaning relatives often come in here to tell people in your father's situation... I don't know... let's see. That so-and-so is dead, or that they're having money problems. It's understandable, yet totally selfish. They do it to make themselves feel better, but it only causes further trauma. And besides, their loved ones forget it all a moment later anyway, and all that remains is a lingering sense that something is wrong, but no knowledge of what that something is. We want to avoid that. We must not judge your father by the same system we judge ourselves. OK?

I dabbed my eyes with a tissue, stood up and said, more harshly than I meant to, *Yes. Right. I've heard all of that. Can you help us with the tea now, please?*

But the Sister didn't get annoyed. She continued just the same. She'd seen thousands of people like me before, desperate to leave her office. Not really listening. Not coping.

Someone will see to it, she said. *They'll probably be waiting for you when you get back to the table. The kettle is constantly on here.*

And they did arrive before me. Two piping hot teas, safe and secure on the table, in white plastic cups. It was beautiful. I could have cried.

Dad was deep in thought when I returned, and it took him some time to notice me. But eventually he looked up and said, *Oh, there you are. You left me on my own! You took me away from my friends and then left. You know I can't move without help! It's all fercockt around here. Nobody cares about me.*

That's not true, Dad. I'm so sorry — it was the nurse's fault. She wouldn't let me go. And I'm here now, isn't that something?

He thought for a moment, then his expression softened. *Yes. Yes it is...*

Good. Well, I have something to tell you.

That's fine. Don't worry about your old dad, I'm really

OK. Good Jewish people here. Another, more troubling thought occurred to him. *Half the staff are bloody foreigners, though. From Poland, Nigeria, God knows where else — alle schwarze yorren basically — but I'm OK. I survived the war, I can survive this nuthouse! And you're here now. Which is more than I can say for your sister.*

What?

You've always been a good boychik, I know that. But that sister of yours... He shook his head, as if he could hardly bring himself to speak. *Don't tell her I said this, she'd be devastated, but what a waste of space she is!*

I felt hot and clammy. I wondered if anyone would notice if I just got up and ran away. I thought about reminding him gently, lovingly; saying *I am Deborah, Dad* — sparing both of us whatever he was about to say.

Did you hear she's running away to Israel now, to fight in the war? On the other side! Jews are fighting Jews now! She's killing her own family! She hasn't come to tell me, but I know. I have my sources.

I think you're talking about your own sister, Dad. Elly. Remember? She worked in a hospital in the West Bank for a long time — it was a good thing she did — she puts the rest of us to shame. People were dying. They still are.

People are always dying! Your grandfather must be spinning in his grave, God rest his soul... They'll never accept her over there you know — she'll be hated by both sides. Is that what she wants? To be hated by everybody? Ducking for cover as the bombs fall? She could get herself killed!

She had, but I couldn't remind him of that.

Please, Dad, listen. I, er, Deborah... she's not gone anywhere. But she will be doing, soon. She's moving. You won't be seeing her for a while. She's finally happy — isn't that what you always wanted? She's very much in love with a man who —

Is he black?

Why? Does it matter?

If he's not black it doesn't matter at all!

Well, he's not. He's a good man, and he loves her. He's definitely leaving his wife soon and Deborah is moving to be with him. They're going to live in a little town on the south coast. It's very attractive.

I'll never see her again if she goes there. Never has been peace between us and the goys. Especially in that place. There never will be. What arrogance to imagine you can just make it burst out of your pupik. Poof! Magic! Peace! She doesn't understand what she's doing. She's going because she's got no children of her own so her heart bleeds for everyone else's.

And then I said what I came to say.

Sorry, Dad, but I just can't come back. Will you forgive me?

I began to cry, but he was so far away in his own thoughts that I might as well have been somewhere else already. He was warming.

All that time we fought for a homeland, all that time wandering in the desert, he wailed, his face contorting as if he was transported back sixty-five years, standing at the entrance of the camp again, dreaming of freedom. *And she wants to give it away! She spits on six million dead! My own child! But you're a good boy. Speak to her for me. She listens to you... Oh, when I think of all the friends I lost. The worst crime in history! Oh, oh...*

He began to weep too now, but I couldn't console him. Though I'd promised myself that, whatever happened, I wouldn't get angry today, I stood up and shouted, *You have to forget your war! You never let anyone forget it! Look — I'm trying to tell you something about me — just shut up for a second —*

Tired once again, my father wiped away his tears with a damp palm and composed himself. He seemed to get sudden bursts of energy, then lose it, then regain it again.

Sit down and behave, he told me. *Have some respect. Who do you think you are? Those bastards would push us all into the sea if they could and you know it.*

Who? Who are you talking about?

I tell you, when Martin Luther King was killed, do you know what I did? I bought a round of drinks! Another one bites the dust. Boom! Do you see what I'm saying to you?

No, Dad. What's that got to do with anything?

They say he's President of the United States now. Doesn't matter! Nothing ever changes! Filthy niggers... they hate us. Everyone does. They pretend that they don't but they do. They'd drive us into the sea if they could —

DAD! STOP!

A few of the other patients turned round to see what was happening as the Sister arrived and put an arm around my shoulder.

That's enough now I think, she said without looking at me, then smiling at Dad as if she was talking to a child. *Isn't it nice for your daughter to come and see you? Your daughter Deborah? It's good to talk over old times. I'm glad you've had a lovely afternoon together. But say goodbye now. It's time for Deborah to go.*

This seemed to jolt him out of previous worlds and into a new one. He looked into the middle distance for a moment, processing the information, then looked at me as if for the first time.

Ah yes, he said. *My daughter — little Debbie. Good of you to come and see your pa. Good girl. I remember when you were born... such tiny hands. But strong. You held my finger so tight! I love you, dear. I love you so much. You know, David is getting married today. Isn't that nice?*

I felt a strong pain in my gut. I wanted to tell him David had got married twenty years ago, divorced ten years ago, and that I was leaving. But instead I just gave him a kiss and said, *Yes, Dad. That's lovely.*

I nodded at the Sister then walked away, noticing both cups of tea remained untouched. That detail upset me more than anything. I hadn't even managed to stay with him, be good, for long enough for us to enjoy a single sip together. As I reached the automatic doors I heard Dad say to the Sister, *What's for dinner then?*

She explained the menu in full, a waitress in an exclusive restaurant, and he explained he was going to make a complaint. Standards had been slipping recently, he said. There was no excuse for it. Did she know he survived the war? Did she have no respect? Why wasn't he being treated properly? When was he going home?

I left the building. He was her problem now.

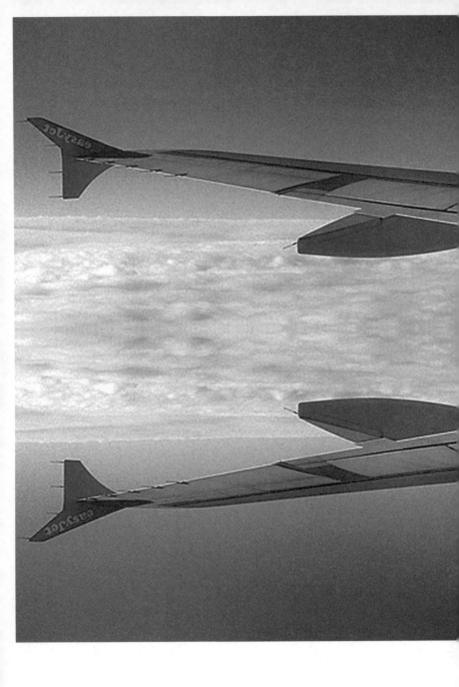

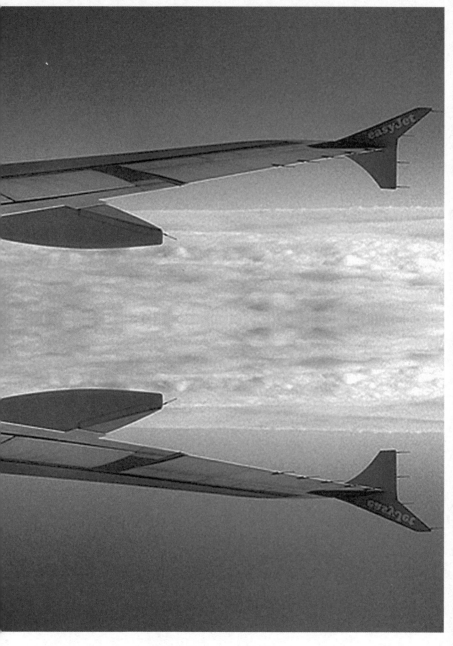

Kõik, mis ma ootasin, et anna mulle rõõmu ja mis [...] veenis mind läbi teekond oli mulle pettumus — aga välja, et väga pettumust, olen omandanud ootamatu haridus.

INTERVENTION

Towards the end of the flight I think, *when I arrive tonight, I want to find our home ransacked. I want to find our stinking bins emptied out into the front garden and your dirty washing tipped into the snow by two fat men in balaclavas.* I think, *I'd like to stand on the street, hands streaking my cheeks, in front of neighbours who don't yet know the news. I could run inside, followed by rubberneckers, and open my wardrobe. There I'd find my shirts shredded, my fingers buried in the damage as I held the stringy leftovers close. I could open your wardrobe. See what you'd left behind.*

The plane sinks downwards, swerves, and the headline is I'm still here. I don't get sucked into the air vents above my head or down into the engines below. Even though right now I'm last night's cheap wine, last night's slip on the ice, though my head is a washing machine with a rock in it, they say I've been keeping to my schedule perfectly. Carrying out plans made when I was another man. In the circumstances, that sounds unlikely. But then, they say we're *flying* here, and how likely is that? Hundreds of us, all easing so comfortably onwards, smooth breaststroke through clouds, London to Glasgow in under an hour. Most of us have forgotten we're not secure. We're considering buying discounted aftershave. But when it's offered up, I can't make my mind up about the Allure — I've not slept in a week and I'm leaking out through my pores. Maybe my skin is my only remaining organ — it's the only one I can see — and if it's all I have, then maybe I shouldn't swamp it in chemicals.

I've thought for too long. The duty free floats past.

The pilot is talking about speed. The man next to me is beyond wasted.

The man says he's coming home too. He's singing, *Enjoy yourself, enjoy yourself, it's later than you think,* bumping his head against the seat in front with every other slurred word. This song has only two lines so he has to keep repeating them. Eventually he breaks off to ask if I'm taking the piss. If I've got a problem. To tell the air hostess that this miserable dickhead won't sing along, and it's a very easy song, and we all have fucking problems you know. I can't talk to him, or anyone. I'm about to ask the man to breathe on me, to get me drunk in one toxic blast, but the air hostess cuts in. *Stop bothering the nice man,* she says. *He's not being unreasonable.* I smile at her, cross my legs and look out of the window. It's getting dark out there in space. Soon, we won't be able to see anything.

I turn back, watching the air hostess slide through the aisle, talking behind her hand to a male colleague as she moves. He glances my way and shakes his head as if to say, *There's always one.* He gives me that *aw mate* smile I've had a lot this week, and he answers the air hostess in a whisper. Then he turns and refills his trolley while she whispers into the intercom. All this time she's eyeing me as if I'm some bone-skinny cat with rescue-me eyes and three legs and I'm thinking, *I haven't even done anything. I've been burgled in my sleep.* I watch her lips move and fill in the sounds like I know what they are. Like I've ordered her to make them. She's saying, *Derek, remember to rip the radiators from the walls and hurl the computer through the window. But do it with love. He's still in the forgiveness stage.* They can arrange that you know, even at short notice. Customer satisfaction is everything. They can find a specialist, be with you quicker than a plumber. And you don't even have to be in when they call.

The man is snoring now and I'm thinking I'll be on the floor tonight. Before this trip, I slept on the couch — Tuesday, Wednesday, Thursday. The bed lay stripped, untouched. With any luck, neither will exist any more.

The plane is making its final descent. Inside, only the reading lights remain, little alien beams in the black, and outside, those clouds have become thousands of laminated houses in the distance. The houses are surrounded by laminated fields with laminated hedges encasing them in neat laminated squares. Everything is clean and in order.

As we lurch downwards again, the air hostess comes to check we have our seat belts on properly, our iPods and iPads turned off. There's a shake somewhere in the belly of our machine as she walks by, but this woman has seen everything. She looks at me saying, *You're going to be just fine,* and right then I want to pull her towards me and lick the make-up right off her face. She must know what I'm thinking because she leans over and gives my hand a light squeeze, her warmth fizzing up my sleeve, down through the buttons of my shirt and into my jeans. I'm surprised I'm capable of feeling this, and wonder what else I'm capable of. It's getting rockier now. The plane shudders and jolts, waking up my man who begins to sing again. *IT'S LATER THAN YOU THINK!* he spits, at no one.

As he's singing, beating the chair with his palm and

trying to rouse a few supporters, I tidy my things away into my rucksack, thinking, *after this journey ends I will arrive at the airport, and no one will meet me. I'll stride through the airport lounge to baggage reclaim. The assassins will work while I'm waiting for my suitcase to drop onto the belt. They're professionals. As they shatter the light bulbs we bought, I'll get healthy food in for dinner from the airport mini-supermarket, maybe think about repairing the bike that's been rusting in the hallway,* all this as I choose between near-identical bundles of asparagus.

While I wheel my suitcase to the taxi pick-up point they'll be daubing our walls with graffiti, the filthy insults in big letters, primary colours, in thick block characters. As the taxi heads out onto the motorway, our furniture will be chopped up and put through the grinder. They'll be efficient, these men. Their stomachs will be straining to burst out of their skins. By the time the taxi pulls off the main road and onto our street they'll already be halfway to the next job, a warm glow in their chests and several piles of sawdust in every room. They'll tell dirty jokes as they leave, inflate as they walk, then at the end of their shift they'll go home to get a hard-earned treat from their loyal wives. Everyone has a wife. I notice that now. And when I put the key in our lock I'll find it smashed.

The door will swing open, I'll stand in the hallway and hold myself in. Maybe I'll stand there for hours while friends queue up on the doorstep to touch my shoulders and tell me there's nothing I could have done. I'll not scream or punch the floor. They'll say my spine is still so straight, my gaze is like a lighthouse, they can't believe it, and I'll nod and tell them I know. I'll be thinking, *thank God they burned our filing cabinets. Now I won't have to divide the paperwork.* Then I'll pace through our hallway, coat still zipped up, clocking the dirty bootprints in our bedroom, the vomit in the sink, the globs of mud in the bath. I'll notice the bed is gone, already broken up and sold on in parts, and I'll birth a secret smile, letting it out through one of the broken windows. My friends will be looking elsewhere.

Allt som jag förväntade mig att ge mig glädje och som [...] övertalade mig att göra resan hade besviken mig — men av just besvikelse har jag fått en oväntad utbildning.

ORIENTATION #2

At this exact moment, as visitors to The Eternal City will notice upon arrival in the Piazza del Popolo, the bells of the Church of Santa Maria are ringing. A wedding is taking place inside. For the guests this sound may be joyous but the noise means protestors on the square's South Side have to strain their voices to be heard. *Yankee E Sionisti Sono I Veri Terroristi!* says the banner being held up to the sun by five lean figures surrounded by two hundred more, many of whose faces are painted in the colours of their mother country. The chiming seems to be getting louder.

From the banner alone some distant observers may mistake this for a pro-Palestinian rally, but those paying attention will notice images of President Assad (known as the Lion or Duck, depending on your politics)[8] revealing the true cause being fought for here. Dozens of Assad faces on sticks bob in the bright blue of the Roman afternoon, his fatherly expressions a contrast to the ones Westerners see when the Syrian leader is cartoonised back home. Here in this corner of the ancient city, flags are waved with gusto. Children are shouting loud. The women are quieter — but then, they're standing by the security. At this exact moment, visitors looking to the left will see a policeman spitting on the ground and saying to his colleague, *So tell me, how is this Obama's fault?*

On the North Side of the Piazza, a different scene can be observed. Several elderly Americans, weighted with bags and jewellery, are taking turns to photograph each other in front of the vast obelisk Napoleon pinched from the Egyptians back when this place was still called France. In front of the monument, see how Maisey from Long Island is giggling — she thinks the obelisk looks like a massive penis — and who can blame her? But visitors to Rome, both liberal and conservative when it comes to matters of the body, won't hear her mention this to her friends. Instead, she's posing sexlessly for the camera, making a V sign for peace in the same spot where, for centuries, public executions were held. She's unaware of

---

[8] President Bashar al-Assad's supporters have called him The Lion, but leaked messages between Assad and his wife Asma revealed her pet name for him as 'batta', the Arabic word for 'duck'. This detail went viral in 2012 and was adopted by Assad's enemies, who labelled his army 'Assad's Duck Brigades', chanting the taunt in street protests, designing cartoons of the dictator and even dressing up as ducks as a form of satire.

this, but Maisey's V is hovering where the once-feared guillotine used to do the same, just before it plunged into enemies of the Republic.

If visitors stand close to Maisey they might take a moment to consider the nineteenth-century writer and social critic Charles Dickens (1812-1870). In his travelogue *Pictures from Italy*[9] Dickens documented a Roman beheading witnessed during a time when, in dark moments, the great man wondered if the guillotine might be coming down on his literary career.[10] Demonstrating his undoubted talent for a gruesome scene, Dickens illuminated the experience in a way that will surely speak to those visiting the city over a century and a half later, describing how the murderer (or executioner, dependent on your views on capital punishment) lifted the disembodied head by the hair, presenting it to the crowd before wedging it onto a pole for flies to feast on. In this moment, the audience saw the dead man's eyes turn upward, as if facing a nearby crucifix. *Every tinge and hue of life had left it in that instant*, wrote Dickens, of the head recently liberated from its shoulders. It was dull, cold, livid, wax.

---

[9] Though representatives of the Estate of Charles Dickens may dislike it, readers will note that Pictures from Italy 1844-5 (Bradbury and Evans, 1846) is now available for under £1.50 ($2.35 US, 1.9 EURO) in Penguin Classic edition on the Amazon Kindle.

[10] Sales for Dickens' previous novel, *Martin Chuzzlewit* (Chapman and Hall, 1844), had been poor, and the reception to the preceding *American Notes For General Circulation* (Chapman and Hall, 1842) had sometimes been vicious, leading the author to fear both the public and critics were turning against him.

These words will surely prompt sensitive visitors to this famous City of Fountains to ponder the value put on human life, both in the then and there, also the here and now. Perhaps Bashar al-Assad might want to think of Charles Dickens next time he's sending out his Duck Brigades to put down rebellion amongst the poor and the desperate. Perhaps he might imbibe the life lessons embedded in *Oliver Twist*. But why dwell on scribblings from a bygone era when discussing the current political reality? Dickens is long dead now — dead as the condemned man in his description — while Maisey from Long Island is alive and smiling. Behind her, visitors will see that actors playing Mickey and Minnie Mouse are also alive, though sweating heavily in body suits. They play up to passing tourists, handing out flyers for today's Disney matinee. Tickets sales have been sluggish. They're under pressure to deliver.

To the right of Mickey and Minnie, the Statue of Liberty decides this might not be a profitable spot after all. The protest is affecting business. So she unfreezes, removes her crown, lifts the day's takings and heads for the next square. She's been working this City of Seven Hills for two years. If you ask, she'll tell, *she's giving it one more, then it's home to Oregon. Her mother will understand.* A small boy passes while she ponders her options; he holds a giant balloon in one hand and grips his father's leg with the other as he gazes up at this creature in green and white. The unfrozen Statue sees him and sticks out her tongue. If visitors look closely, they'll observe the boy letting out a half-laugh, the string tugging free at the moment he forgets himself. Then he remembers, and looks upwards. The balloon is in the national tricolour and it says *ITALIA* on the side. It escapes the Piazza del Popolo and swims into infinity. Look up, visitors to Rome! Watch it shrink and rise. Tonight, when all this is history, it will join the stars. The balloon will do things mere people can only dream of.

The church bells cease and the wedding party crowds onto the steps, a swarm of stylish bees in tailored yellow and black suits and frocks. Despite the competition in the Piazza, visitors to this country's grand capital should feel lucky they picked this day to make their trip rather than that Easter week they dithered over for so long. Magic is everywhere. See how the respective mothers of bride and groom have forgotten their year-long feud; how they start crying at the exact same moment and throw their arms around each other, causing a ripple as one by one the congregation realise the consequences. *That's what weddings are really about,* whispers the bridesmaid to her visibly pregnant sister, who was not asked to represent the family today. Both younger women also start crying, though neither knows why. Visitors who witness this tender exchange should show a little respect. Go over. Give them a hug or something. You might be an outsider in this country but you're still a human being.

Standing on the Church's third step, the groom cradles the small of his new wife's back and tips her like a kettle, kissing her in triplets for the crowd — one, two, three, rat-tat-tat — and several of the guests break out into song, drowning out the protest on the South Side of the Piazza. You might not be able to make out lyrics but you can follow a melody, and everyone knows the sentiment, right? What, have you never been to a wedding before? Stand still. Take in the scene. Turn off your fucking phone for once and be at peace. If you believe in love, you might even want to close your eyes and wait for a cold shiver to penetrate you, despite the searing heat. The French can say what they like. They usually do. But Rome is the real city of romance.

If you want to see the Caravaggios in the Church of Santa Maria, you'd better be quick about it. In the commotion, sneak up the side of the steps and in the entrance, though traffic will be heading the other way. When you've passed through the mounted skulls and multiple Madonnas that clutter the front entrance, once you've passed through the pews and admired Raphael's 'Creation of the World' up above on the dome, you'll reach the paintings that really matter. These are on side walls at the back, as if trying to remain hidden from those who don't appreciate real art. The priest may say there's no time, there's another wedding on soon and you have to move move move, but if visitors take off their garish hats, cross themselves and promise to be *solo un minuto,* they'll be able to persuade him otherwise.

So steal a moment or two with Caravaggio's masterpiece 'Conversion on the Way to Damascus', also his 'Crucifixion of St Peter', before the priest ushers you out of the cloistered viewing area. In order to get the most out of the experience, look closely, and breathe slow. You might be an atheist but so what? It's still worth contemplating. The desperate figure of St Peter will remind some visitors to Rome of the fragility of human dignity, others of the cruelty of Christ's torturers, who knew so little about the compassion he preached. It was a different world, even to that of Caravaggio, a man rumoured to have used corpses as his models. Let's face it, even Silvio Berlusconi would have been horrified by the chaos and corruption that led Jesus onto the cross. Before leaving, be sure to take in the splendour of the Church of Santa Maria, and be thankful for being born in your own time.

On your way out, be an ethical tourist. Make a donation to the upkeep of the church. Buy a candle or something. Then move on.

Back outside, keen observers will see the protest is growing, but it's not really possible to hear it clearly. The Piazza is large, noise is swallowed by the sky, and the wedding party is too loud. Also, homeless Andrea is right behind you, and no doubt he'll be wailing about damnation, as he often does at this time of day. Unless you dodge him, he'll be in your ear as you leave the church, eyes on your wallet. Visitors to Rome are well advised to not think about Andrea, or the millions like him who look just a bit too much like St Peter on his cross. Move away, and don't dwell on the protest either. Most people here don't care about Assad the Duck. Why should they? Like Tunisia and Bahrain before, they'd not even heard of Syria before all the recent publicity.

Instead of wasting time on politics, visitors should look in the other direction and open their hearts to the true beauty of Italy. Inhale the glorious architecture, wonder at the Latin carving on the walls of the Piazza behind the wedding party and sneak a look at the young lovers under the arch, kissing deeply for the first time today. Even experienced travellers cannot fail to be touched by the spirit of Rome — but you'll be pleased to hear you're now finished with this corner of the city. Walk away without looking back. Next up it's the Coliseum, then three other stops this afternoon. You've got a dinner reservation at eight. You'd better get a move on.

By check-out time tomorrow morning, these images will be memories. Visitors will open the blinds in their room, look out onto the bright, open street, breathe in the smells of the café below and find it hard to believe there's a war going on anywhere.

Semua yang saya harapkan untuk memberi saya kegembiraan dan yang [...] memujuk saya untuk menjalankan perjalanan telah kecewa saya — tetapi daripada kekecewaan yang sangat, saya telah memperolehi pendidikan yang tidak diduga.

WE'RE ALL GONNA HAVE THE BLUES

I reckon it'll be late autumn, heading into winter. That time of year when Europe goes black long before the end of the working day and people walk home by lamplight, eyes on their shoes, umbrellas held out like shields against the wind. In the November cold even life's winners grip the rail on the underground or the tram, coats damp, wondering what they might have done with their best years. Jaro says it's all about temperature drop. About smells too. *The physical is everything,* he says in that low growl of his, as if what he's saying couldn't possibly be disputed. Jaro tells me that even if people don't know they know it, most folks can sense darkness coming. Their bodies can. Their brains. And this is when he sees it happening, at the back end of one of our bleakest days, the water steadily rising, creeping up on us like old age. No big flash of light. No earth-shattering crash or bone-shaking split. He says it'll probably start all quiet, while we're both here, far from home, amongst the doubters of Eastern Europe.

Where I sit right now, at a low table in The Jazzrock Blues Bar in Krakow, underneath the low brick arch,

I'm waiting for Jaro to show. I usually hold off on my first grown-up drink till he appears, but this day has felt like a week and the fat old bastard was supposed to be here half an hour ago, so fuck it. I get myself a beer and sit back down at the moment the Magda Octavia Quartet float on stage to the pitter-patter of warm applause; as they pick up their instruments I count six of them. This seems an important detail. Perhaps because I did eighteen hours yesterday, I was up five hours before polls even opened today, the night is climbing all over me and my mind's beginning to run. Jaro says that's okay — he says that wherever I am, it's the running mind that's got me here — but these days I mostly dream of just lying still.

I sit at my table and sip, and swallow, and as the music starts I wonder why there are six people in this jazz quartet, and wonder where the fuck Jaro is, and then I become convinced that this is how it's going to be: it'll begin in a place like this, on a night like this, the floodwaters lapping at the door then suddenly breaking through. Beata, our Glorious Leader, wrote in this week's email to all staff that *together, we can hold back even the strongest tides,* but then she's bound to say that — it's her job to ignore reality. She was born for this game of ours because she

1. doesn't change her mind about anything,
2. doesn't like travelling to explain that, and
3. Is senior enough not to have to.

But instead of dictating a letter, sending an email or God forbid picking up a telephone to get things done, she ruffles my curls, promises me treats for good behaviour and sends me bounding across the Channel, into the corridors of not-much-power, tail wagging and tongue hanging out, messages tied to my collar. My task? To sniff the arses of those at my level, then persuade them to go home and bark at their masters that no matter which Party wins the election, *it's really about time they opened their hearts to the movement.*

Most of us younger generation know appeasement will fail. Right now we're busy appeasing all over Europe, in Germany, France, Switzerland — in jobs where all sensible tactics will have no impact until it's nearly too late. Jaro understands this. Say what you like about him but the man has a good nose for the brown stuff. *First you need to eliminate poverty,* he told me last year, on my 21st birthday. *Then crime. Then cellulite. Then maybe we'll get people's attention. But in the meantime, we're fucked.* He forked a meatball and swallowed it in one go. *Still, at least we can die knowing we were the kind of losers who never gave in to the Dark Side.* There's another reason Beata keeps me on permanent duty in Krakow: to babysit a man twice my age, who talks like the Star Wars trilogy is a series of historical events. In recent months, that man has decided he wants to move to Poland for good, to *live in the land of my people.* (His ancestors are mostly Lithuanian.) In recent weeks, he's talked about giving it all up. He's asked me what I think it might be like to die in a flood. You know — what the sensation of choking on water would actually feel like.

There are about fifty seats here in The Jazzrock, and they're nearly all taken. At the front are the local regulars, each sitting cross-legged and nodding solemnly like they're receiving some news they've been waiting for their whole lives. In the middle rows there are several lone men. Some middle-aged tourists. Elsewhere, a few groups of friends in their thirties and a younger couple who might be on a first date. I'm at the back where two wasted teenagers are dancing as if they're living on another planet which is doing just fine thankyouverymuch. The first number goes round a few times, Magda's saxophone is carrying the melody, then she calls out, off-mic, *Helga Emmanuelle everybody!* and the torture begins. Helga the piano player is first to get a solo. The drummer is second. The percussionist is third, battering the bongos like he's going to break right through their skins. He gets everyone clapping along — there are even a few whoops. I get up and go to the toilet, pissing at the urinal with one hand on my hip, one thumb and forefinger pressed hard on my nose, trying to remember how I got here. I think about where Jaro might be. I rub my eyes, check my phone and remember there's no reception down here. Then I wash my face with cold water and return. The bongos are still centre stage.

I speak to Beata every day. While she's busy in Brussels, a place where decisions are usually postponed but occasionally made, she tells me she needs someone she can depend on to look after *our special boy,* the big thirsty kid who's somehow keeping us all afloat almost entirely through force of charisma. (That and rich rock star friends who empty their pockets whenever His Majesty does his little donation dance.) I know I shouldn't bite. I know I should play nice. It's just that I don't believe in guardian angels, I've been sleepwalking for weeks, I can't remember a time before Jaro, and even drunk I can't imagine life after him any more. Jaro lives behind my eyelids. He's under my fingernails. I wake up at night thinking he's sleeping in the road outside the hotel, about to get hit by a car. In this job, you get used to thinking about the worst case scenario, so perhaps all this thinking makes sense. But still, it's emptying me out, there isn't much of me left and every night I waste hours thinking about what I'd say to Beata if Jaro jumped naked from the Debnicki Bridge into the Wisla on my watch. *He was a great man, but as frail as the rest of the human race*. Or maybe, *People loved him because he was both the best and the worst of us*. Or some other shiny lie. Excuse my tone. It's just that these days I seem to spend half my life sitting in bars with no reception, listening to eight-minute percussion experiments and waiting for my boss to show. I'm sure he's dead, and that soon we all will be. Sometimes, when I try to picture the big day coming, this big water day he's always talking about, this is how I see it.

It'll be a bit like now, after a big day on the job, but with Jaro actually here. We'll be at this table, deep in the future, my head fit-to-burst with the sound of his never-ending force in one ear and the screech of yet another fucking saxophone solo in the other. After the band finish, Jaro will try to persuade me to stay later, his hands picking away at the candle wax dripping from the bottle in front of us, his eyes tiny red dots in the near darkness as he tells me about this new barmaid who works the all-night shift, that he says has eyes like lollipops. I'll remind him he falls in love with Jazzrock barmaids about three times a week. The way I imagine it, he'll answer, *Look, Zyg, I like happy endings as much as you do, but these fuckers, these elect-a-holics we have to deal with every day, are afraid of their own voters.* He'll say, *And unless they start listening to us soon....* Then he'll draw his finger across his throat. *So let me have my lollipops at night, okay?* Then the water will burst through the door, rising fast up the walls, turning the Jazzrock into a swimming pool, then a fish tank, then a prison. Jaro and me and the girl with the lollipop eyes will know what it feels like to choke on water. I look around: there are no windows in these underground clubs, and we're here three or four times a week — so the chances are, this is where we'll be when it happens. Jaro says jazz helps him think clearly.

It just so happens that the mixture of Tyskie beer, jazz

and all that clear thinking also makes him want to, as he puts it, *appreciate the beauty of the female form.* But for those that think they know where this is headed, I can tell you, Jaro isn't your tenner-in-the-panties type. He just likes to watch the barmaids slink back and forth in their domain while we talk and listen to the band. Occasionally he'll make light conversation, but no more. He says he likes imagining being young, single, free, and living in a world where he has time for affairs. He says his wife doesn't mind. And most times, after a drink or two at the Jazzrock, all that clear thinking just makes him want stagger back to the hotel room and play Osama Shootout on the Xbox until he falls asleep with controls still in hand. For those of us in the business of keeping Jaro breathing and out of prison, this represents another dodged bullet. Last night, I put him to bed at 3am. I took off his shoes and pulled the covers over him. I got water, made him drink some and he mumbled, *The thing is, Zyg… you've got to sympathise with people's mistakes. Their reasons. If you can't sympathise in this job, it's only fair to retire.* Then his head sank into the pillow and his body turned to jelly. Sometimes I wonder, if I told Beata what the face of our campaign was really doing out here, would she drag him home and lock him in her cellar? Replace him with a sober clone? Or, would she just shrug, smile, and remind me who's in charge?

I look at my watch. Then the door.

We usually travel together. Or, I suppose, I usually travel with Jaro, dealing with all the practical stuff so he can, as he puts it, *concentrate on the bloody macro, amigo!* That's his way of reminding me he's still the guy on the posters and the TV adverts. The one people are thinking of when they pledge their donations and set up their direct debits. Jaro is a cash machine for the movement. He's a ghost. He glides from commitment to commitment, seeming to be everywhere but never quite being anywhere. He's making it look like we're progressing, and that means, in financial terms, we actually do. But in private, the progress isn't exactly consistent. One minute he's running around the office and screaming, *We can still do this!* — the next he's got head in hands and saying, *I swear to God I'm going to kill the Chancellor of Poland.* Meanwhile, my life is becoming increasingly fucking *micro.* I carry the bags. I hold the passports and the tickets. I pick him up, tell him where he has to be and why he has to be there, order the taxis to and from meetings. Before those meetings begin I have to make sure Jaro's tie is on straight so people take him seriously. It's not quite why I joined the movement, you know? I even carry super-strength chewing gum in case he's had an early start on the happy juice. Sometimes I pop a piece in his mouth when he's not paying attention. If Jaro's mind is buzzing, his mouth hangs open, inviting the flies.

He's now an hour late.

In quiet moments, Jaro admits he's sliding. Most other times, he denies it. In the car today, on the way to our first appointment, suffering with a stinking hangover, Jaro said, *Ten Tyskies a night is the only sensible response to the current reality.* He said, *Do you know what we've done to our planet?* I straightened his tie again then he shrugged me off and pointed to the skies, crying out, *Listen to me Zyg — never mind the fucking tie. Straight ties are part of the fucking problem!* Times like this, he sounds like some kind of crazy preacher. The sort of drunk you'd cross the street to avoid. The kind of person who goes about screaming that the end is nigh — and no one's gonna believe that now are they? So it's no wonder Beata sends him everywhere with a chaperone. If I was his boss I'd send a fleet of them, and I'd pick better ones than me. I wouldn't even think about the cost. I'm no accountant, but surely to God he could go down on the spreadsheet as a legitimate business expense.

After another five or six numbers, each punctuated with lengthy break-it-downs, squeaks and squawks, the band finally give my ears a break. Magda walks off the stage, straight to the bar, tossing her long tightly curled hair as she orders a large bourbon. The barman asks, in English, if she's heard the election result. She answers, in a slow Polish-American drawl, that there are no politics in her world. No lies and no compromise. Only the eternal beauty of sound. The barman tells her she's full of shit and reminds her she's back on in ten, but despite everything, for a few seconds I think about asking Magda to hire me. I reckon I could play maracas or something. Dance. Fuck it, I could be on *vibes* — I wouldn't want much in return. Perhaps a handful of Zlotys or a few Tyskies each night, that's all, to play and to just be free. I may have spent years running from these sounds, but for a moment I think that maybe they belong in a different world, where *essential policy change* is a phrase nobody needs to use.

The door does not open. I'm still alone. Maybe I always will be.

Mostly I shadow Jaro, so it's possible to keep close by, but sometimes I'm scheduled to do my own thing. When I'm not babysitting Beata's money mountain, I have coffee meetings of my own, and lunch meetings, and afternoon drinks. I get twenty minutes at a time, or fifteen, or ten, with people who all seem to think I hold Jaro's ear in my pocket. Lobbyists and consultants. Assistants and special advisors. Even the occasional Minister. I dizzy people with talk of conservation targets, energy efficiency and climate change. (Jaro tells me to talk fast. After all, we don't have long.) I tell them what we — what *Jaro* is trying to achieve, on behalf of us all. I cajole and persuade. I shake hands in the way he taught me to before the drink took hold of him: firm but not dominant. Confident but not arrogant. I'm sure to turn up on time, smile, be polite. People can damn the system all they like, but these details are the difference between success and another wasted hour. In my meetings, I tell people we need to rescue our future from the profit motive. (I mean this.) I always use the names of the children we need to rescue it for. (The offspring of whoever I'm talking to.) Back when he used to still give me advice, Jaro used to say you should personalise as much as possible, to maximise impact. So I personalise. I ask politicians how their kids are getting on at university, school, kindergarten, then focus on our core targets. But these fuckers say things like, *Where's the man himself, Zyg?* Or, *Why don't we get a face-to-face?* Or, *Oh, look out, Justyna! Here come the Green Nazis!* This is how my world works. I hear other worlds run along similar lines. No wonder some reach for the bottle.

Magda kisses the barman on the mouth and tells him not to worry. She tells him he'll feel better tomorrow. Then she returns to the stage and reaches for her saxophone. She holds it like a newborn.

Before the music starts up again I sink the rest of my drink and go back above ground, back out onto the street, waving my phone about for a while, trying to get the magic white bars to show on the display. It takes a while but finally the thing comes to life: no messages from Jaro, and when I call him it goes straight to answer phone (he's probably jumping off that bridge right now), but I do have an email from Beata reminding me that, today of all days, it's important to stick to the list. Her email also includes a revised schedule for tomorrow, based on the latest set of projected results sent to her from HQ in Gdańsk an hour ago. She signs off, *It wasn't glamorous being in the*

French Resistance either you know. I think Beata knows what's coming. I go back inside and sit down again. I order another beer, wondering if, when the water comes, we'll be able to hear it before we see it.

The last time I actually saw Beata, we met in a hired meeting room in Brussels and she told me about my new assignment. Didn't she know who I was, I asked? Didn't she think I was a little overqualified to be a babysitter? But Beata doesn't have time for messing around. She said, *Your problem isn't qualifications, Zyg. Like everyone else on this continent, it's distractions.* Back then, the movement were still speaking to both sides of this particular electoral distraction. Waiting for the winner to emerge, still pitching to everyone. This last four or five days, there's only one side whose calls we even bother to answer. The people might not have spoken yet but we have a pretty good idea what they're gonna say. Polls close in an hour. They might as well not have opened at all. Anyway, when Beata gave me this assignment she handed over a list titled *THINGS YOU SHOULDN'T LET JARO DO BETWEEN NOW AND THE END OF THE WORLD*:

1. Thou shalt not let him talk policy detail.
2. Thou shalt not schedule meetings before 11am or after 7pm.
3. Thou shalt not let him sack anyone, or hire anyone, without prior written approval.
4. Thou shalt not let him go on midnight jogs *to work off dinner.*
5. Thou shalt not let him drink more than two beers a night. (Whoops.)

6. Thou shalt not let him take drugs, even if he says they are merely *performance enhancing*. (Double whoops.)
7. Thou shalt not let him frequent all-you-can-eat buffets.
8. Thou shalt not let him have more than three consecutive hours of *alone time*.
9. Thou shalt not let him fall in love.
10. Thou shalt not frequent late night clubs. Remember: scandal could strike anywhere, and WE NOW ALSO REPRESENT A NUMBER OF CHILDREN'S CHARITIES.

I asked Beata if she had any suggestions about things two powerless men trapped on a dying planet *could* do in a strange city for nights on end without getting drunk, wasted, talking politics or trying to get laid. But Beata just gave me that look where she's all eyebrows, and I've been working out here ever since. Sometimes I wonder what all this is for. If they actually need Jaro any more. No, they need him alright. All of us do. We just don't necessarily need him alive. The thing I don't ever say to anyone is, *Imagine what we could do with a dead figurehead.* I don't say it because I reckon Jaro's already thought of that.

The band finish another song to the sound of raucous applause. They start another where Magda sings about her Mississippi sweetheart leaving her, walking on down the road and never coming back. She's singing about how she wishes she wasn't so lonesome, in an accent which lurches between Texas and Warsaw. Then she starts up with the sax again.

I think, if only Jaro wasn't the way he is.

I haven't mentioned recent events to Beata but these last few days of the campaign, our man has been displaying what she calls *the classic signs*. He's been missing meetings and getting drunk first thing in the morning. Hiding from me. Talking about his wife, how she deserves a better life, and how his kids don't understand him. How they don't even fucking *recycle*. The closer we all get to you-know-what (and he's convinced we're pretty fucking close), the worse it gets. *Democracy's great for people who aren't bothered about the apocalypse,* he said. *But what we need is a dictator, and quick.* This afternoon he measured his pulse every five minutes and asked me (again) what I thought would happen at the end of the world. Without giving me time to answer, he told me he was betting on the Noah's flood scenario, and that it didn't matter which Party won any more, here, or anywhere. He asked me to keep a secret: that after the results, he was gonna give up the game for good. Buy a hut on top of a hill and hope the waters didn't reach him. Then he shouted, *But first we're gonna celebrate the end of our latest mission! See you at eight.* It's now half past nine, and I'm thinking, *maybe I should have mentioned this to Beata after all.*

Magda is really warming up now. Between numbers she's telling a story about the town she grew up in, her father's old Etta James 45s, how she fell in love with jazz, and how really jazz music — how *all* music — is just the blues with more notes to muck around with.

I can see the end more clearly now: I'll have a pretty fucking similar version of the headache I've had for the last two months, and like right now I'll be alone here in the Jazzrock, in the crowd, imagining Jaro's death and how I'm gonna explain it to Beata. Then I'll see him walking towards me. He'll be drunk, dripping from the rain, and crying about the life he could have had. I'll sit him down, buy him a Tyskie and tell him we've been doing important work. That he's needed, he's a man people look up to, that

I look up to, and that even if the odds aren't good, it's important not to go over to the Dark Side. While I say this, all I'll be able to think of are the costs. After a silence I'll say, *Hey, listen. It's jazz time, amigo.* But he'll shake his head and say, *No, no, it's blues time, Zyg. Soon, we're all gonna have the blues.* Then the band will start up again and he'll get up, to dance alone, just like those teenagers up the back. *Na zdrowie, amigo,* he'll say, still dancing, holding his glass to the sky. *Cheers. L'Chaim. Slainte!* Jaro will smile as if he's forgotten everything. The responsibility, the future, what we all know is coming. Then we'll clink glasses, and the water will burst through the door.

But nothing ever happens the way you imagine it.

Jaro finally arrives. He's smiling. He apologises for being late — he says he lay down for five minutes and woke up two hours later. He's in a clean shirt and looks pretty fresh. He pulls me in close and hugs me. *Whatever happens,* he says, *we've done an honest job.*

We watch the band for a while in near silence, then take stools at the back of the bar, so we can hear ourselves better. Jaro is glowing. He says, *Oh Christ, I love these places! Even the bass player gets a solo, you know? This music, it's a musical fuckin democracy.* He says this as if democracy is what other forms of music desperately lack. As if democracy is something he values. Then something in the brickwork distracts him and he changes the subject. *They've got no fire exits in here,* he tells me. *So if the water bursts through the entrance we'll all be equally fucked. We'll all go down together.*

I say, *Maybe the band will play on as we rush for cover, like they did on the Titanic.* But Jaro laughs and says that's just a myth. He says, *Amigo, we'll either drown as one, or more likely try to claw our way out, fighting each other, trampling on the soloists and the portraits of Louis fucking Armstrong while making for the door.*

Our voices rising over the sound, we discuss what we might do next in our lives. I admit having no suggestions. *I kind of figured this would be a lifetime's work,* I tell him. Jaro leans in and says, *It won't be obvious it's coming, Zyg. Before it happens, everyone will think we're crazy for telling them what's on its way. We're not talking about a hurricane here. No machines have been invented yet to predict this. But I can see it.* He closes his eyes and keeps talking, but lower now. *It starts with a trickle of water through the drains,* he says, *swelling up at the sides of the streets. There'll be a slight rumble in the sky, but no more. And people won't see it coming. They couldn't. They won't know what they're looking for. They'll be going about their business, thinking about their boyfriends and jobs and holidays and sick relatives. They'll be running for buses. Worrying about their tax bills. Having affairs in unnamed hotels and wishing they'd made it up with their father or mother before they died. And why not? You've got to have love for the people, amigo. You've got to forgive what they do. Something will always seem bigger, until the second before the water bursts through the door. And when it happens? You really think the band will play on? Or you think they'll panic and eat each other?*

Jaro sees my expression and retreats.

Actually, maybe it won't happen at all.

He leans back and grins. Our table shakes slightly.

Or maybe it's about to happen right now.

Then there's a sound at the top of the stairs, by the entrance to the club. A force pushing against the door. The band seem to be getting louder. Then they go silent.

We all look around.

Allt sem ég bjóst við að gefa mér gleði og sem [...] sannfært
mig um að taka að sér ferð hafði vonbrigðum mig — en út af
þeirri vonbrigði, ég hef keypt óvænta menntun.

THE HIPS ON PLANET LATINA

After peering through the darkened doorway to see what kind of place this was, he decided to go in. Anthony stepped off the street and felt a jolt in his gut. Then he leant into the chunky glass block which separated him from the world on the other side. The door was heavy. It began to shift.

Once inside he stood in the purple light bathing the doorway and breathed in through his nose, smelling smoke. Then he let go of the door and watched the glass begin to slip back. (This is how it seemed, like it was slipping.) The hole belonged to this building he'd walked by eight times in the last fortnight, but tonight was entering for the first time. On a Friday night. Way past nine o'clock. Here he was a man without a history, nobody knew his profession, and this could be *his kind of place*. He hitched up his jeans by the belt, and why not? Tomorrow night Tunisia would be in the past and he'd be back on the couch at home, complaining about the cold. His eyes adjusted to the lights. They were low enough to make his skin seem darker but bright enough, perhaps, to show off the shirt he'd haggled for at the beach that morning. The shirt had a certain effect. It still had what his wife called *that fresh-from-the-designer-sweatshop smell.* If she'd seen his top two buttons undone she'd have teased him, and the two of them would have kissed. As he thought this, the door finally closed, as if in slow motion. It seemed appropriate. This was the *High Flyer Brasserie.* It wouldn't do to have doors close in a rush.

Anthony looked around at the well-groomed bar tenders, chefs and waiters sitting at the surrounding tables. He wouldn't notice this sort of thing, but the *High Flyer* was where these people came after working back-to-back double-shifts. After days of bowing, grins fixed on their faces, hoping for disproportionate tips from those who'd not yet worked out the value of the currency or were too rich to bother calculating it. Many spent 60 hours a week or more saying *please* and *thank you* in Italian, German, English, French, always making the effort to guess the customer's mother tongue and switch to it without comment. Doing all this regardless of whether it was deserved, wanted or noticed. Not that Anthony would even consider these sorts of details (he was already far off in his own thoughts wondering, mostly, why he was experiencing the beginnings of an erection), but the *High Flyer Brasserie* was the only venue where these workers from the food stalls and the town's endless *tabac* stands, these children of quiet, religious men who'd grown up on these streets and now wore sunglasses at night as a statement directed at their fathers — *this* was the only place these people felt free. These people, who shunned tradition and spent their only day off in full-on rebellion, these were mostly young men. Because in this town, the cooks, waiters, servers and stall holders were nearly all young men. It was a young country. It was a male country.

Anthony had seen this for himself during the last fortnight, which he'd mostly spent travelling between customers of his own, taking orders from big warehouses and corner shops and family businesses. As he'd joked to Caragh on the phone, apart from the odd pensioner in a head-to-foot white shawl, he had hardly laid eyes on a female the whole trip. So he couldn't have played away if he'd wanted to!

He picked up a menu and scanned the contents.

The prices in the *High Flyer* determined the clientele. Drinks were just about affordable for locals, being lower than the town's tourist bars but higher than average, giving what its American-born manager called *an air of exclusivity, a unique space*. The *High Flyer* was off the main track, somewhere locals whispered about, kept to themselves. It served beer with alcohol in it. It was open till dawn. And, as Anthony was just noticing, it even hosted the occasional *woman*. Ones whose dresses showed flesh above the ankle and below the neck, who wore tight jeans, dresses and high heels, who smoked, laughed and drank with the men like they were staking a flag in newly-discovered land they'd been inching towards for centuries. The bar here had fluorescent pink lines underneath which suggested something exciting — these lines zipped round the outskirts of the service area and flew off, unafraid, into the distance, as if making a break for foreign shores.

This place, with its English-only sign out front, understated private booths and Western channels on plasma TV screens, this place let local boys and girls play at being wealthy Westerners — ones who just so happened to prefer Arabic music, and who happened to sell chawarma and pizza by day. It let them be, for the night, extras in The Sopranos. Each town waiter, now being waited upon, felt the weight of the beer bottle in his hand and surveyed the scene with satisfaction, imagining himself as a central character in a film with a dramatic, happy ending set in a country he'd only experienced on DVD. Not that Anthony was even listening, but here, sons of fishmongers dropped words like *babe* and *dude* into their conversation. They modified their accents. The *High Flyer* was far from the sober café culture that pervaded this town, this country as they saw it — the sausage-fest, plastic-chair-and-table coffee places on every corner which only served espresso and chichas and hosted men who hadn't had serious hopes in decades. Who hated their leaders but never tried to change them. Within months, the sons of those men, the very same ones now in the *High Flyer Brasserie*, would put down their drinks, rise up and wake the whole Arab world. Soon they would reach up and tear down the pictures of Ben Ali on public walls, the ones looking down at them in every shop or café window, and smash the last forty years, demanding freedom. But not quite yet. Not tonight. For now, that revolution was only just beginning to bubble, and between these walls the only system belonged to a distant land, one they wanted to reach out and touch. As Anthony noticed, the seats here felt soft. They promised something. The blinds kept the outside world firmly out (or hid disapproving eyes looking in) and that was the way customers liked it. The *High Flyer* preserved the illusion of being at the pulsing centre of New York or LA right up until closing time. This was the management's unspoken promise.

Anthony was aware he'd been standing for too long.

He picked a booth in the far corner with a view of the whole place. This looked like a spot for a successful businessman. Someone taking some deserved *me-time* after a day's serious work. So he strode over and sat, sliding his backpack out of view in the same swift movement. (Backpacks were not welcome here, it was obvious. Even ones containing sales reports from recent days that Walid would be very, very pleased with.) This table had a clear view of seven television screens running in tandem, on silent, while to the right of the largest one he could see three older men in good suits, deep in conversation. They looked different. They had bellies suggesting decades of success. Anthony straightened his back, stretched, and tried to work out what channel he was watching. He wondered whether these guys were the management. Then he thought, *perhaps this was a brothel.*

Local music played through the speakers. To Anthony it sounded like religious dance music, though he suspected this guess was based on a Westerner's prejudice. (He slipped into that sometimes. He knew it.) This sound, it certainly had the cadences of religious music, the instrumentation, the wandering lilt of the call to prayer he'd heard from his hotel room, wafting across the street from the mosque. Curiously, this perhaps-religious song was being delivered by a man making no pretence of being able to actually sing — a man whose tone seemed to say, *this is just my job mate, I could just as easily be an oven salesman* — but people were nodding along to it as if finding something delicious and wicked. And actually, Anthony noticed, it did have something of that to it. A lightness, perhaps. A darkness. A sound that hinted at something filthy going on, somewhere close by. As Anthony settled in his seat, thinking he'd finally *discovered* something on his travels, not merely *visited,* he observed some of his fellow customers more closely. Some small groups. Two large ones, mixed gender. Couple of drunks. A few younger men, like him, sitting alone in the near darkness. But — as Anthony noted with pleasure — they all looked like locals here. Locals keen to suck up this experience as if sucking up the future, which they believed, he imagined from their expressions, was wild, and dangerous, and uninhibited. It was a future that didn't care about the opinions of others: it was wearing impractical suspenders and probably crotchless knickers. (Or *panties,* as the Americans say. And these fellow customers of his, it wasn't London, Edinburgh, Cardiff or Belfast they were dreaming of.) A man at the next table nodded, as if sharing something. Then he looked away.

The three suits at the bar were moving their hands, and Anthony wondered if they were discussing a drug deal. (They weren't.) As he considered the details of the exchange they might be engaged in (but weren't), speculating about whether it was smack or crack or something else they were smuggling (or weren't), and thinking about just how dangerous that kind of life might or might not be, the lights changed colour and the music in the bar went up. In an instant, the atmosphere changed. The volume of this music suited the sort of place where bare skin was standard currency on the dance floor, clothing merely the optional, occasional decoration around exposed legs, arms and torsos. Here, there wasn't even a dance floor at all. And yet, it seemed like there was. Something was going on. A music video started on the screen, a new song blasted through the speakers, and three off-duty waiters at a nearby table recognised the tune. They stood, raised their glasses and clapped along, one attempting a sort of drunken belly dance. Anthony recognised the dancer. He'd served him a crêpe two hours ago.

Just then, someone new appeared at his table. This person was dressed like everyone else. It didn't seem like he was working. Actually, thought Anthony, did *anyone* here act like they were working? What did this individual want? A light, perhaps? Did he want Anthony to leave? As if answering these questions, the standing person cocked his head upward, and Anthony said, *UNE BIÈRE S'ILVOUS*

PLAÎT. Which seemed to be right, because the person grunted then walked towards the bar. Anthony smiled at this reaction; he was in possession of a strange power. He leaned back and drew his arm across the chair next to him as if there were someone sitting in it, Caragh perhaps. No one noticed this. He shifted in his chair again, wondering how people behaved, alone, in bars with loud music in the background. Then he focused his attention on one of the many screens. A woman was dancing, wearing a bikini Caragh might have described, with acid on her tongue, as *basically a piece of string attached to three cheese triangles.*

He had now been at the *High Flyer Brasserie* for nearly three minutes.

He watched the bikini woman in the screen.

One thing was obvious: this woman was not from this world, or even from Anthony's world, but from what his brother Barry called *Planet Latina,* somewhere Anthony had never visited but had heard much about. Barry had lived on this planet for a while, a place that, whenever asked, he liked saying was *anywhere south of Texas, baby.* Barry holidayed there often, always coming home looking tanned and well-fed and strangely confident. In unguarded moments — in moments, basically, of drunkenness — Barry explained it was hot and poor on Planet Latina, and full of women scouting for Westerners. These women dreamed of resettling in cold countries, where they'd be happy doing cleaning jobs and performing explicit sexual acts for white whales like him without a thought for themselves, as long as they got a passport out of it and could send money to their families. These women were angels, Barry said. They'd rescued his wavering belief in God. He said that, in the hope of escape, many of these gorgeous, angelic women — and here was the crucial detail — many of them would gamble on putting out for a night or two, on the off-chance. This was what Anthony had heard about Planet Latina. And, though he knew Barry was full of shit even at the best of times, though Barry was basically ignored or laughed at by everyone he knew and though Anthony was an intelligent enough soul who knew a made-of-crap male fantasy when he heard it, he enjoyed, just for a moment, imagining capturing this woman in the video and taking her home with him to Bexley Heath in a sack, tied up with the string from her bikini. He didn't want to hurt anyone. The idea horrified him. But in the imagination, he thought, who gets hurt? He was just waiting for his drink. Anthony wondered how long it would be till it arrived. This place was having a surprising effect on his imagination.

The world slowed.

He felt a dryness in his mouth, a bead of sweat on his neck.

Watching this woman move, this shiny-skinned, slender woman surrounded by several half-naked boys mirroring her actions, Anthony realised it had been two weeks since he had seen a belly button, either on a screen or in real life, and he'd forgotten the magic of it. This belly button danced, and the hips either side of it danced too, shifting in a kind of symmetry. He wondered whether she'd been operated on. If she had, he didn't want to know about it. She was singing to him, *at* him, her fingers making a *c'mere* signal, a cheeky smile on her face which looked entirely spontaneous and gave Anthony a tingling feeling he wanted to bottle and keep. (In reality, the woman had been required to offer up said smile, for hours at a time, on several separate shooting days. During the filming of the video, her fourteenth, she'd reproduced it repeatedly as if she'd just received some fabulous news. She did this is nine different costumes. She did it in three locations.

In a private moment with her PA, she complained that all this posing and pouting made her feel *more like a whore than an artist* and said that from now on she was going to take charge of her career. Her next record was going to be a concept album in Spanish about her ancestors.)

The news the woman in the video was pretending to be so delighted about was unclear, though Anthony imagined she'd received a passport in the post. He laughed inwardly at this, then stopped because actually, he had no one to share the joke with, and *she* was the one in the television, while he was an oven salesman sitting in a bar looking at her virtual stomach. (He looked.) In that moment Anthony realised, with another jolt, that he would probably leave Caragh if he believed he had a realistic chance of licking that stomach, just once. He wondered what else he was capable of. Then he wondered if, armed with this new self-knowledge, he'd ever be able to return to his quiet suburban marriage. Meanwhile, the woman's hips continued to shimmy, surrounded by members of her large and supportive local community, all partying like, actually, it was fine. There were no problems. Isabella (he called her Isabella) looked perfectly happy on Planet Latina. Anthony couldn't imagine why she'd want to leave, and began to wonder whether Barry had really visited this place at all. He thought: *Where was his fucking beer?*

Just then, the camera cut away to a muscle-bound black man delivering his lines to the camera. (He was conscious of registering the man in the screen as 'black' rather than as just a man. It was the kind of thing Caragh, whose father was Jamaican, and who prided herself on her Caribbean roots, criticised him for.) It looked like this man was rapping, but Anthony was now worried, *perhaps that too was a racially-based assumption?* (It wasn't. The man was actually rapping.) Then the video cut back to Isabella

again. And then back to the man. He'd clearly invested
a fair chunk of his life in a gym, this man, and acted like
he had no outer body confidence issues. Isabella had spent
time in the gym too, lots of it, and also looked supremely
confident, though obviously, as Caragh told her husband,
all women had body issues of some sort, no matter how
apparently carefree their shimmying hips. It was just a
case of how well they hid it. On this screen, now — female
belly button, male chest. Belly button. Chest. Belly button.
Chest. Then a wide shot of the sea. Then Anthony's beer
finally arrived, a cool wet bottle which somehow seemed
luxurious. The waiter presented both items to him just like
he'd taken the order, as if really he wasn't a waiter at all.
Anthony didn't see this but he sensed it as he watched
the screen, wondering for a moment whether there was
some arrangement, some understanding, between workers
and customers here that he hadn't quite worked out yet.
(Yes, there was. And no, he hadn't worked it out.)

The thought passed.

He was back on Planet Latina.

The narrative of the music video had moved on since
the arrival of Anthony's beer mere seconds ago. What first
appeared to be a simple party duet was now developing
into something more like a mini romantic drama. In
one shot Isabella jumped onto the back of a motorbike,
holding onto a strange waist, a different one to the one she
was sharing the song with. Next she was at a beach party,
near some expensive cars, while the biker rode alone,
distracted. Then she was back in the city, getting changed
into leather boots in the street, and then they were together
again, the couple, in a tight clinch, as if they loved each
other faithfully and deeply, and knew they always would.
They kissed. It looked convincing. (When introduced on
set, the two actors disliked each other instantly. Isabella

told her agent she'd rather die than risk disease touching this individual — she'd heard he was a womaniser whose conquests numbered in the thousands. The man considered changing his agent. He'd done proper acting work now, he wasn't just a model, and was conscious of the imbalance of his CV. But they were professionals, the two of them, and they got on with it. Besides, they were both attractive. And in the end, kissing each other was easier than expected.)

After the clinch, the motorbike rode into the distance with both of them on it.

Anthony sipped his beer. It tasted good. He looked around the bar, but not for long. His surroundings seemed less interesting now.

In the next segment of the song, the climax perhaps, Isabella looked like she was in yet more mini-scenes with *lots* of men who were perhaps the same one but perhaps not. None of them seemed to be related to the rapper, who was now a less regular fixture on screen. (This was not explained.) Anthony thought, *what was the message of this video?* Perhaps simply that Isabella from Planet Latina was very sexy, and very horny, and potentially yours. You, the viewer. Perhaps the point was that, as a star and therefore public property, she belonged to *everyone*, really, even the guy performing the song with her — though surely no one seriously believed that, outside of the mere fact of celebrity, these two had a single thing in common. They lacked screen chemistry. (For starters, they appeared to have filmed their parts on different continents.) Anthony, who was given to outbursts of indignation about small issues he felt represented bigger ones, had a thought that made him feel drunk, even though he was still on his first beer. This song, he thought to himself. The existence of it. It stank of strategy. Straddling two international markets by gluing together bankable names who'd open up crossover potential to the other. The song was irrelevant. The hip-shimmying was a cynical ruse, to hypnotise. Anthony pictured the board meeting where the idea was hatched, and was disgusted. The screen cut back to dancing at the beach, with plenty of zoomed-in torso action. Specifically, zoomed-in hip action.

Another beer appeared at his table, unbidden. He drank it.

These hips were getting a lot of screen time, but despite his disgust, Anthony was prepared to tolerate them a little longer. (He had now entirely forgotten what country he was from, also that he was sitting in a small bar in a minor town on the coast of Tunisia. He had even forgotten, briefly, that he was married to a woman he worshipped, and that he was a really rather successful, passably attractive oven salesman attached to a medium-sized firm making serious inroads in a country where it was possible to purchase an oven at midnight.) Anthony thought, *what did it matter anyway, all this? What did it matter if he stared a while? He couldn't be blamed for watching one of these many screens in a context where, let's face it, there was fuck all else to do except watch screens.* This bar, as far as he could see, had been specifically designed so men like him could sit in booths and watch hips jutting, grinding, bouncing and swaying harmlessly in the ether until they were ready to go home. (The men, not the hips.) Besides, this singer, the one responsible for this virtual strip show, this singer was probably a millionaire. She probably had a handsome singer husband who probably also kissed strangers on screen for a living and mimed along to songs written by others. So really, where was *his* crime? Also, it had to be said, these were exceptional, mesmerising hips. Astonishing hips. The hips of a goddess. Skin wrapped tight at the bone on either side but with just enough wobble at the belly, the tiniest fragment of wobble, to hold the attention of any viewer regardless of age, nationality or sexual preference. The hips on this screen in front of him, Anthony realised in a moment of unusual, startling clarity (he was often confused), had the perfect combination of tautness and wobble. Surely even Caragh — a woman who prided herself on her intimate knowledge of the physical defects of famous people — a woman whose manic displeasure at the sight of other female bodies was almost pathological — surely even *she* could understand that. (He thought: He wanted to call her. It was her smell he missed the most. And the way she cuddled into his back at night.)

As the thought of Caragh's unique smell drifted away and the contents of the video drifted close, Anthony's imagination began to take him elsewhere. He thought that, really, these hips were hips to finally crack the Middle East peace process. To unite the fucking world, you know? When you considered the issue properly, these hips (he looked), these hips, and all hips like them — or even not like them at all! — were, essentially (he kept looking), all of human history. Perfected. Sculpted. *Condensed.* They were the *universe,* these hips. They were the *reason* for the universe — the reason human beings had not died out. Because, you know, people had looked at hips like that and been compelled to procreate. Was that not true? And if it *was* true, was that not a thing of incomparable beauty? (In the background, his soundtrack — more humming keyboards. More crashing strings and rapid tabla thumps.) Was it not his duty, as a living breathing oven salesman, every bit as essential to human history as anyone else, anywhere, ever — was it not his responsibility to admire these hips as you would admire Michelangelo's David or the Mona Lisa? (He'd seen both of these works of art on family holidays as a child, but had not been impressed. Meanwhile his erection was now, at last, complete.) This idea, of these hips representing all of human history condensed, being the universe, the galaxy, the stars and Milky Way, the past, present and future of all experience, struck Anthony as tragic and deeply poetic. In his mind it was the answer to all questions, the question to all answers. As he thought, he realised this thought right here was possibly the only truly interesting or original or important thought of his life so far, the only one he might ever have, and he was overtaken by an urge to write the thought down before he forgot it. Which he knew he was likely to do. In fact, which he knew he was *certain* to do unless he got to a piece of paper and pen pretty fucking smartish. He searched his backpack.

He found paper easily enough but could not find a pen. The video ended.

As he looked for the pen, a new video began. This one was filmed live at a concert, featuring another impossible, unattainable, possibly surgically-enhanced Arabic version of Isabella, only wearing a less revealing outfit. Despite showing less leg, she was somehow more alluring.

As it played, Anthony noticed the waiter who served him the crêpe swaggering past in the direction of the toilet, wearing a shirt very similar to his own. The waiter, called Rached, who was also an accomplished poet, nodded in acknowledgement, but with a new confidence. Perhaps he was smirking. (He was not.) This thought troubled Anthony. Perhaps he was being laughed at. (He was not. Simply by *being* in the *High Flyer Brasserie,* he'd gone up in Rached's estimations. Besides, Rached was a nice guy and often smiled for no reason.) Anthony stopped. He went back to looking in the rucksack. He wondered what he was looking for. And then, through no fault of anyone's

— neither his nor Isabella's nor Rached's nor anyone else's — the thought about the galaxy was gone. It had arrived without warning and left the same way. Anthony mourned the loss. Already, he missed the magical hips from Planet Latina, and the poetry contained within them — whatever it was — which was now gone forever.

His erection subsided.

He wanted to leave.

He looked around once more, wondering whether maybe there was only one place like this in town because everyone else was perfectly happy with life here, and maybe they didn't need any more *High Flyer*-style brasseries. Maybe there was only just enough custom for one.

At this moment Anthony really wanted to phone Caragh, who he really did love, he always had — he felt like calling her and trying to explain all about this evening he was having, this few minutes of discovery and loss which was probably changing him in ways he didn't even understand but *she* probably *would* understand because she knew him better than he knew himself. He was desperate to phone and say he missed what she smelled like. (She would consider the comment odd and ask him if anything was wrong.) But he was powerless. He couldn't. He was alone with these thoughts because tonight she was with a friend, and rules had been clearly laid out. She'd warned him that her phone would be off, all night, because the friend's husband had just left her for some penniless Ecuadorian twenty-something slut who was clearly just chasing a passport. They were having a girls' night in, just the two of them and several bottles of wine, and the last thing the suffering friend needed was for a *man* to call during the conversation and remind her that the woman consoling her, the one telling her she was right there, sharing the anguish, and that it was all going to be okay, the last thing this poor friend needed was a blatant reminder that this *consoling* friend was actually perfectly happy in her relationship thankyouverymuch, and that, at the end of the night, after the compulsory drunken hugs and declarations of eternal friendship and statements like *all men are bastards, who needs them?* and the heartfelt appreciation for such a special night which she was convinced would really help her *pull through this difficult time,* the last thing this poor lonely woman the wrong side of thirty-five needed was the knowledge that the person who appeared to be right there with her in the struggle was now free to go home, kick off her shoes and text her husband to tell him how proud she was of him working so far from home, all alone, selling ovens to provide for their future. This desperate, lonely woman would not want to be reminded that her friend was probably going to message her loyal, adoring husband from bed that very night, in cutesy text-speak, to say that as soon as he returned she was going reward him for his responsible behaviour by fucking his socks right off.

Now would she?

Desperate though he was, when it was put that way, Anthony understood why he couldn't phone home. And it was just this kind of thinking ahead regarding the phone situation, this attention to small practical details, the caring for others, which was typical of Caragh. As he considered this he held his beer tight and went numb around the toes, just as he had done the day they'd met at Barry's garden barbecue, the day when the storm came so quickly that they'd all had to run inside, already soaked by the time they made it to cover, each holding bowls of damp salad and smiling natural smiles. Anthony felt a pull on his cheek muscles and noticed he was smiling now too. He looked forward to going home and kissing Caragh's belly button.

This desire was the only thought left in his head as he sipped some more of his beer. (Though the reason for it escaped him.)

Just then, as quickly as he'd been taken over moments before, Anthony's attention was stolen by something moving at the door of the bar. A stranger, a tourist perhaps, one hand pressed over her forehead, looking through the thick glass door, just as he had a few minutes ago. She peered inside, perhaps to see what kind of place this was. The tourist was looking at the screen, then the bar, then the seating area. She appeared to recognise something. Then Anthony smiled, gesturing for the stranger to come inside. It was okay, Anthony seemed to be saying. In here, in the *High Flyer Brasserie,* everything was okay.

Tout sa mwen espere, ban m 'plezi ak sa ki [...] pran tèt m'
nan antreprann te vwayaj la wont m '- men soti nan desepsyon
trè, mwen te aprann yon edikasyon inatandi.

59 PLACES
TO FUCK
IN ARIZONA

There's been more time to study her since the tribunal, but you can't do it twenty-four-seven. Some people in this world still have jobs, and Jennifer's boss would hit high C if she found out you'd been trailing round after her in the ward. Sampling the tablets. Asking dumb questions. Pulling her into the supplies cupboard for a quickie while some war vet was spluttering his last on the other side of the wall. No — once you're struck off in that business, you're struck off for life. And not all Jennifer's ideas are good ones.

So for most of the last three months you've limited your study to home hours, entertaining yourself in the flat alone while she's been out at work. You cooked prawn linguini with chillies the night you were sacked, vegetarian lasagne the next. The whole first week you hoovered and dusted like a demon. Jennifer called you her bitch and you laughed together. She predicted your periods would synchronise soon; she made you pinky-promise to run her a bubble bath whenever she demanded it. That was when you were still buzzing from the freedom and every task was fun — then the role-play started. Now, some nights, when Jennifer's on duty, all you do is cup your balls inside your trackie bottoms and make plans online, in the darkness. *At the Lowell Observatory in Flagstaff,* you mutter to yourself, clicking the mouse with your free hand. *At the Saguaro National Park near Tucson.* Just thinking about it makes the back of your neck wet. Your mouth dry. When it all gets too much, you revert to mastering FIFA 12.

Whole nights pass this way.

It's been four months since the management asked Jennifer to cover a couple of night shifts as a favour — one of the new girls was off ill, they said. It was just till she felt better, they said. Probably wouldn't be more than a week or two. But it's nearly Christmas now, the ill girl has become the *depressed* girl, and Jennifer's still on these nightmare lates with no sign of a pattern change any time soon. You hoped that once you were out of the call centre it might mean a chance to discuss starting again, perhaps somewhere life was cheaper and the sun was more likely to shine. But there's been no time for that sort of talk. Six times a week she leaves home after sunset and gets back before sunrise. Day is night and night is day. Jennifer says it's playing with her senses, and it's affecting yours too. You're having to adjust your sleep patterns just to co-ordinate being awake at the same time. *On the Apache Trail, overlooked by the majestic Superstition Mountains.*

You make sure you're ready when she gets home from work — lights off, blinds shut — so Jennifer can kid herself it's night-time. She deserves a proper welcome home but you've learned not to bother her at the door. She doesn't like to be fussed over. What she does for a living, you can't imagine it. The last moments of ordinary men and women, stripped of themselves. It's no wonder she needs a few minutes alone. So you lie there in bed, pretending to be asleep, listening to her move in the kitchen, picking from things in packets in the fridge and eating standing up as night becomes morning outside. Then she'll crawl into bed, kiss you once and fall asleep, sometimes fully clothed. If that happens you undress her slowly, careful not to make any sudden movements, removing her make-up with a face wipe. You put her bra, knickers and tights into the washing basket, and hang her uniform up on the back of the bedroom door ready for the following day. Then you pull the duvet over both your bodies, run your arms round her waist and wait for tiredness to take over. Most times Jennifer sleeps deeply. Sometimes you do too.

Jennifer's dreams don't clear her mind, but when she opens her eyes she acts like the world is a shiny new penny she just found on the pavement. Most days she'll wake up around two, roll over to face you and before you've even focused she'll whisper, *Shall we, cowboy?* When she's tired, her pupils look like roulette wheels. When she's horny, she wraps her short legs around yours, holds you hard and asks you what it's gonna be today. Barack and Michelle in the Oval Office? Beyoncé and Jay-Z in their LA mansion? Brangelina in their South of France hideaway? Usually you decide together. Then it's dress-up time, half an hour of what Jennifer calls *rock n' roll in the same old holes,* and by three you're both asleep again. You wake around five, crash in front of the TV and grab a sandwich while watching the soaps or a DVD. A couple of hours later it all starts over, and the next ten hours are your own.

Last week you told Jennifer this couldn't go on anymore. They were taking the piss, these suits, and you advised her to go on strike. It wasn't practical, this sort of life. You told her that, if it went on till Hogmanay, there were gonna be problems. What were you gonna do for the bells, eh? Sky Plus the whole thing? Watch Big Ben the following afternoon, all lights off, singing Auld Lang Syne and pretending it was a different year? Jennifer wrinkled her nose. The corners of her mouth turned upwards. Then she said, *We should get busy during the countdown. Try and co-ordinate. You know, 3, 2, 1…* Jennifer's a real romantic. These past few weeks, you've noticed some things you didn't see back when you had a job and still picked up the phone when it rang. If Jennifer's sleeping, you concentrate on her breathing, trying to echo it with your own, wondering if she only stays with you because she's too exhausted to leave. If she's awake, you pay attention to her tics and habits. Her desires. You still have some uses, right? *In the disabled toilets at the Sea Life Aquarium in Tempe. In full Native American costume at the Heard Museum.*

From the timings, you know she hardly ever makes a stop on the way home from work. The thin layer of wet mud on her boots proves she always uses same the same shortcut through the park — the route takes around twenty-three minutes, door to door. The *played* count on her iPod shows she listens to the same albums while she's en route — full-up *Born in the USA* on the way to work, empty *Nebraska* on the way home. (She only listens to Springsteen these days. She says he's written all the songs she ever needs to hear. On this issue, you disagree.) There aren't many shops open on that route at 6 a.m. but anyway, even if there were, you doubt she'd stop in anywhere before coming back to her man. Her Daniel. Jennifer's a pretty regular girl. The numbers speak for themselves.

Give or take a few seconds, Jennifer spends thirty-seven minutes getting ready for work every day — you know this because you have a stopwatch on your phone. That thirty-seven minutes usually includes about eight to get dressed, two of which she spends putting on the jewellery you bought for her birthday, for Valentine's Day, for last

Christmas. It includes six-ish minutes for her daily bowel movement. Three to brush her teeth. Nine minutes to put on a little blusher and eyeliner. Then she usually spends four or five discussing what you plan to do with yourself while she's feeding, bathing and changing what she calls *the drooling zombies of Yorkhill*. It's hard to think back that far — it was when you first got together, two or three years ago now — but when she started at the hospice, Jennifer was softer round the edges.

Back then she talked about doing *work that was good for the soul*. In company, it gave her a certain glow. Now the two of you don't socialise, she tries not too think too much, the patients have become the *zombies*, and at home it's all dressing up as Hitler and Eva Braun and pretending your flat is the bunker, allied bombs raining down from the outside as you squeeze in one last desperate lay before the pretend suicide pills kick in. From what she's told you about what goes on in the ward, all these behaviours seem like pretty essential survival tactics. Jennifer says that if you think about it, the fantasies actually *improve* the quality of care someone's granny and granddad are getting in their last days on earth. Out there in the world, the fantasies are *saving lives*. So the least you can do is run the odd bubble bath and make sure you get the outfits for a decent price off eBay.

For a few weeks after the tribunal you indulged in conversations about how you'd go about contributing to costume costs, also to more mundane stuff like the mortgage, the gas and electric; you promised to scan the papers for opportunities. You told Jennifer you'd check the job sites and sign up for email alerts. Sometimes you said you were meeting this or that contact for a pint before last orders — most of the time this was a lie, but Jennifer let it go. She didn't ask for details, or follow up afterwards if you said you had an interview at O2, or H&M, or wherever. Still, it was obvious you had no desire to re-enter the job market. Barman. Waiter. Shop assistant. *When you only get one life*, you've been thinking, *why would you bother with any of that?*

Last Tuesday, when Jennifer asked about your plans for the day, you just came out with it: *Remember when we talked about putting a pillow over Auntie Joan in Arizona?* you said, trying to make out her expression. *Taking over her place? Well maybe we don't need Auntie Joan. Look, I've found something.* Then you showed her the site: *17 — At the Arizona Science Centre. 18 — Mid-hike, on Squaw Peak, in the Phoenix Mountains Preserve.* You waited for her to throw something. List the bills she'd been covering since Greg and the guys at Head Office *liberated you from The Man.* You wouldn't have blamed her if she'd left the flat and never returned. But Jennifer's a fucking saint. She's a naughty girl. She wrapped her arms around your neck, her warmth swimming through the air between your bodies, and she bit your earlobe, once, holding the flesh between her teeth for a few seconds before letting go. *Use your imagination,* she said. And that's what you've been doing ever since.

Sometimes you wonder about what life would be like if you'd grown up pre-internet. What did people do? Perhaps they just gazed out of windows or down at their shoes all day, sure there was life out there somewhere, unable to prove it. How lucky you are to have access to every wonder of the universe in a millisecond. With more possibilities for the human imagination than ever before, there's no excuse for boredom. There's a community out there for everyone. *Pigeon Fanciers of the Ex-Yugoslav States. Pumpkin Growers of Yorkshire. Witches and Neo-Paganists of the Deep South.* Some people find so much available information overwhelming. They see the world, notice how small they are, and freak out. But you're one of those who can happily spend the length of an entire hospice shift downloading music for free, watching YouTube videos of hippos dancing, and surfing for unusual places in foreign countries to give the girl you love a good hard seeing to. The universe has its arms open for you both. There's no reason to be afraid. And, as is proved beyond any reasonable doubt by these magical virtual pages, *everyone's* got their thing. The tagline to the website reads: *A home from home for open-minded travellers who appreciate natural beauty of all kinds.*

Number 23 reads: *At dusk, in the remarkable Desert Botanical Gardens.*

Number 31 reads: *In one of the amazing underground caves at Kartchner Caverns State Park.* (Some joker has added a pitch black photo here, captioned 'Inside a Cave'.)

Below the full list of all 59 'Challenge Spots' are links to a series of photo albums, each showing images of couples who have recorded themselves in various places on the trail. Most people don't hit more than ten locations. Most of the images are amateurish. It doesn't matter. One snap, of a couple from Copenhagen, is taken from the perspective of a woman straddling her husband by Lake Havasu. In the picture, you see her knees pressing down onto his arms. He's on the floor, gazing up. This man's expression, it's like nothing you've seen before, and when you show it to Jennifer she wonders aloud what he does for a living. Whether he lied to his boss about why he wanted the time off from work, and whether his workmates know all about his holiday. Then she pushes you onto the floor, a slideshow still showing the couple from Copenhagen in a variety of ambitious positions in Canyon de Chelly, then at the Out of Africa Wildlife Park, then at Old Tucson Studios.

In one video clip they're wearing matching Stetsons, running naked from two Park Rangers. Jennifer insists on doggy style, with both of you facing the computer. She pushes back into you hard.

That was three nights ago.

Tonight, as she was leaving for her shift, Jennifer hugged you tight and asked if you had anything to help her through to break time. You thought about it, eyeing her closely as she picked up her keys, put on her coat and walked out the front door. She started down the drive. Then she stopped on the pavement. Looked back. Leaning in the doorway, seeing her as Marilyn Monroe, you as JFK, you said, *Number 43 — Inside the vast depths of the Grand Canyon, overlooking the spectacular views of what geologist and explorer John Wesley Powell once called 'the most sublime spectacle in nature'.* Jennifer turned back towards the road, shook her head, smiled. As she was walking away she called out, *Someone's feeling freaky today.* Then she was gone, and you watched her go. Your Marilyn. Your Coco Chanel. Your Michelle Obama.

Jennifer always said the first few hours of her shift were the worst, so you made sure she had a text waiting when her first short break finally came round — something to help the second part of the shift pass that bit quicker. It read, *On one of the tables at the legendary Pizzeria Bianco (average Trip Advisor Rating 4.0 out of 5). Feeding each other optional.* You attached a jpeg of Bob and Sue Hampton from Bournemouth, him in nothing but a chef's hat, her as a topless waitress, the two of them busy next to a large plate of antipasti. At ten past midnight the reply came through, *Looks messy. But tasty! I'm up for it if you are…* After that you sent suggestions more regularly. You couldn't help it.

Option 1: IN THE WILD, WILD WEST — 1880s-style, in the famous Rawhide Wild West Town, taking a ride on

the mule-driven Butterfield Stagecoach, which passes
through the picturesque Sonoran Desert. (Other options
include shotgun wedding — cost $10, inc. souvenir photo.
Potential complications: What to do about the guide? Can
you hire your own Stagecoach? And would your mother
mind if we got married abroad?)

Option 2: AT THE MOVIES — In Monument Valley,
dressed as eccentric four-time Academy Award-winning
director John Ford & his beloved wife of 59 years, Mary.
Suggestions: wear an eye patch, as Ford did; reproduce
versions of scenes from Ford's most revered works.
(Possible issues: how to make The Grapes of Wrath sexy?
See also: How Green Was My Valley).

Option 3: SAINTS AND SINNERS — At the San
Xavier del Bac Mission in Tucson, founded 1692. Dressed
as Pastor and enthusiastic member of congregation. (NB:
In a supposed *miracle* witnessed by people from *all over
the Tucson area*, apparently Father Ignacio Joseph Ramirez
y Arellano is believed to have continued sweating hours
after death. He was later made a Saint. Perhaps he could
be incorporated somehow?)

Jennifer didn't answer any of these suggestions but
then, she did prefer dramas where the woman dominated.
Or maybe she didn't reply cos this was stupid and you'd
gone too far and she had no time for this sort of thing cos
she was busy wiping the backside of some frail, frightened
old lady who'd probably have a heart attack right there
and then if she heard what you were planning to do with
her sweet, kind-hearted nurse. Why didn't Jennifer reply?
Something was wrong. It was, it was. Even though you knew
you weren't supposed to when she was on duty, you had
to phone. Her mobile was off. Of course it was off. Instead
of leaving a voice message, you texted her one more time:
I miss you. I'm really proud of you. Come home safe, okay?

She arrived eleven minutes later than usual so you knew something was wrong before you saw her crying. She ran into your arms in the hallway and hid her head in your shoulder, keeping it there for a long time. When she looked up, her face was all running make-up and fear. She couldn't breathe. You said, *Come on, cowgirl,* lifted her off the floor and, waddling along with her raised in front of you, carried her up the stairs. She laughed. You held her softly as she hit you and said, *You're not allowed to go anywhere*. Soft kisses turned to hard ones and soon after you were lying on the rug in the bedroom, facing each other, two bodies in the morning light. *Get me tissues, Daniel,* she said. So you did. Then you went upstairs to run her a bath.

As you did this you thought that if you were still working at the call centre, or anywhere, there'd have been no time for this. Jennifer would have gotten home, dried her tears while you slept, not wanting to wake you before your alarm went off. You'd have woken shortly after, showering and getting dressed in a rush, noticing something was wrong but having no time to respond to it, promising the two of you would talk later. You'd have gone to work, fretted about Greg, about targets, about how much the others in the office were selling. By the time you got home Jennifer would have been getting ready to leave for her next shift and wouldn't want to cause worry, so she would have pretended to be fine, and before you knew it the feeling would have passed. *In Oak Creek Canyon, Sedona. Amongst the birds, animals and plants of the southwest at the Boyce Thompson Arboretum. In Paradise Valley*. No, you never want to work again. You don't ever want to miss being there for her. The thought of it makes you sick.

But it's okay because you don't have a job, you're here, and you're free, and you know the way she likes it so you load the bath with two capfuls of bubble potion, run the cold tap a while first. You fill it to just over halfway. Then you lead her up to the bathroom, take off her uniform, laying each piece down, careful not to crease. She says, *I'm awake for once.* You say, *Yes, I know.* You kiss her collar bone, behind her ear, bend down and kiss between her toes. She pretends to push you away. You let her. All this time she's crying. You pick her up again and put her gently into the bath. She turns from pink to white, the bubbles swarming around her, her body disappearing under them. Then you go back downstairs to the fridge, uncork a bottle of white wine and return, laying both bottle and clean glasses on the floor. *Do you want me to pour?* you ask, and she nods. *Do you want to call your mother?* you ask. She shakes her head. *Later,* she says. Then Jennifer touches your arm and tells you to stay.

You pour two half measures.

With a sigh, Jennifer says, *I shouldn't… I mean, it happens all the time but… Victoria died during the night.* You answer, *I didn't know you gave them names.* Jennifer hits you lightly, laughs, takes a glass and says, *They have names when they arrive, dummy.* And then she starts crying again.

Between tears she tells you the life story of this woman you've never met and Jennifer has never mentioned before. She lived fully, she travelled widely and spoke four languages. She had three children, including one called Samuel that succumbed to cot death. She worked in Polish jazz clubs and once played the piano at the Royal Albert Hall. She lived in Arizona with her second husband for six years before moving back to Glasgow, and told Jennifer stories about her friends and family who settled there after the war. Victoria had seemed fine yesterday, when she complimented Jennifer on looking rosy-cheeked. By which she meant happy. *Not that any of it matters now,* says

Jennifer. *Yes it does,* you say. You ask her questions about Victoria while you're on your knees on the bathmat. You run a sponge softly over Jennifer's arms and legs, then her stomach, then her shoulders, until she seems unable to keep talking. Then you dry her eyes, hold her hand in yours, and take over the talking. You do so quietly.

Here's the plan, you say. *You ready?*

Jennifer nods.

Tomorrow night I'll break into Greg's car, hotwire it, speed over to the hospital and pick you up, mid-shift. You'll stab your shift manager with an infected needle right there in the corridor, then burst out of the doors and jump into the car through the window. Then we'll hit the motorway, making our plans as we go. Number 46 — In the cage with the lions at Phoenix Zoo. Number 49 — On the stairwell of Montezuma Castle, looking through the turrets at the tourists below. Number 53 — Out in the open, on board a boat on Lake Pleasant. You think as you're talking. *Then, at the ferry port, I know a guy, I've planned ahead, and as the sun's coming up I slip him a wad of cash in return for fresh passports. Jennifer says, Where did we get the money?* You squeeze her hand to remind her not to ask questions. *I become José,* you say. *You become Rosita. Then we queue with the rest of the passengers, getting onto a luxury cruise liner bound for New York. On the boat we both face the little round windows, the water, the sea. The heat rises off us. In New York we steal another motor and travel the two thousand or so miles to Phoenix. We sleep in the car. We hold up petrol stations on the way with the gun our man gave us at the port. You're a natural. You threaten the staff and I grab the money from the till. Amazingly, none of these places we rob have CCTV.* Jennifer makes a face but lets you continue. *Only a few people get a cap in their ass, and it's okay cos most of these guys are old anyway, or are bad to their wives.* Jennifer squeezes your hand back and says, *Daniel!*

You smile. *Okay, okay. Anyway. Nobody follows us. It takes two weeks to get to Phoenix but by the time we get there we have a huge surplus of cash.* Jennifer says, *And then what?* You grin. *And then we head off on the trail!*

Jennifer's drinking from her glass, then she puts it on the side and lays her head back on the side of the bath, facing the ceiling. *Sounds okay,* she says, looking at you with those roulette eyes. *But what about tickets for this cruise liner?* You wave imaginary tickets in front of her. *Now. Would I forget something so important?* She snatches the air from your fingers, leans forward and kisses. *I really want to get out of here,* she says, the wobble in her voice returning. *I know,* you tell her. To stop her crying again you raise your glass and say, *To Arizona!* — but you clash glasses so hard that Jennifer's smashes, leaving hundreds of little shards in the bath.

You hold her hand tight and say, *Don't move.*

Todo o que eu esperaba para me dar pracer e que [...] me convenceu a emprender a viaxe tiña me decepcionou – pero por que decepción moi, adquirín unha educación inesperado.

LIBERATION STREET

Beata says it's like rescuing an orphan. Feeding it. Giving it shelter. Wrapping a shawl around its shoulders. *It just so happens,* she says, *that this particular orphan gives me a good hard seeing to five times a week. And you'd be amazed what zest gratefulness can add to a man's lovemaking.* That kind of logic allows Beata to explain away drawing six figures a year from a so-called 'green' charity. The absence of any job at all keeps me floating up and down this yellow strip of a Tuesday afternoon, ordering cocktails and wondering how it's all going to end. Meanwhile, my old friend's face — colourful, youthful, freshly fucked — haunts me as if she were dead. All week Beata has been fighting environmental fires in Poland, bounding between meetings with politicians and strategists, a tigress freed from the zoo. *Stop being so selfish,* her last email said, *and give something back to the world.* She signed off with a smiley face. She's fifty-seven.

Here, I wear the ring you bought me, the one with the narrow score round the outside, on the traditional wedding finger. It took some work to wrench the thing from its old place on what my father used to call *the why-no-wedding-*

yet finger and shift it next door. It had been snug for years. Now the damned thing stares at me day and night, asking questions. *What exactly do I think I'm playing at?* it says. *What have I done to deserve this sudden upgrade?* The ring flops around loosely, threatening to jump down a plughole when I'm in the shower, or leap into the dark when I'm walking back to my room. It's only a matter of time before I notice my hand has no ring on it, and it's too late, and I end up on the mud path back from the beach, after sunset, begging sunburned English whales with whale husbands and screaming whale children to help me look for a ring with a narrow score round the outside. I'd like to pop that ring into my navel like a coin. Have it die with me. Survive long after both of us, lying on its own in a single pot holding our ashes, sucking up the dust. Still, what I want doesn't count for much. I didn't want your skull shattered by a thief either, I didn't want to wake to the sound of it, but no one consulted me over the issue. So I mourn the ring now to save myself the trouble later. And in the meantime it does its job, keeping interested parties informed of my current status: HARD TO GET. By the way, the ring has left an indent on either side of the why-no-wedding-yet finger (even now I can't say it without shaking my head), also a small band of white skin that hasn't seen sunlight since we were teenagers. Maybe I should just move the fucking thing back to where it came from and stop living a lie.

But it's tempting to keep on like this when the lie is leading to new truths. Yesterday, Hassan clocked the ring and asked, *Does your husband treat you well, Christine?* His cheeks are a child's. His eyes are a man's. I answered, *Like a queen.* And I was convincing. No, it's not quite the truth, but few husbands reach two decades' service these days, and no towel boy could make me feel more like royalty than you did, every day, every year. I blame you, Jonathan, for loving me so well. If only you'd slowly crushed me as some men do their women with the passing years — a chilly comment here, an infidelity there, pregnant sighs, broken promises — if only I'd survived all those ordinary things women put up with, leaving them grateful and dependent in middle age, then perhaps I wouldn't be getting cravings now. Half these dizzy widows never had a genuine compliment in their lives, so they don't have to notice the difference. I have no such luxury.

There's not much to discover here. For a start, locals are not allowed in the complex unless they're serving us, so the fixed-grin waiters, our boys on the private beach and the kids' entertainers in orange shorts are the only North Africans I've met in nearly two months of *travelling*. (Amanda thinks that's what I'm doing. I send her emails every few days so she doesn't worry about her old mum.) Also, we're miles from genuine life — the isolation is proudly advertised on the literature like a recent award. The closest thing to a village is the shopping centre, which is a ten mile taxi ride away, too far for most of the whales. They can hardly summon the strength to squeeze into their swimsuits after injecting the all-you-can-eat breakfast buffet, never mind actually brave the outside world. Another guest here told me, with great pride, as if she'd built it with her own sausagey hands, that the shopping centre is modelled on some upmarket Parisian suburb — I had to stop myself from giving her a lecture on globalisation. But but but. Never mind never mind never mind. Even if I don't like what I see on land, there's always the sky, and the sea. As Hassan tells me, his hands in mine and his mind on the future, *Certain things no regime can steal.*

I'm trying to explore my surroundings a little each day, even if that's a victory so small it seems like defeat. Last week I made it to the nearest shop without consulting the map. Five nights ago I reached the restaurant at the far end of the beach without asking for directions. (The website described this place as *a stone's throw* from the sand, but the hotelier must have a ferocious throw or a good imagination. The internet is getting worse, Jonathan. It's home to a hundred million lies and barely a single truth.) I did something else that night too: logged on to the forum Beata told me about, using her password. Would you believe such things exist these days? Are there no police officers in the virtual world?

Well until there are, it's good to know that widows with half-beating hearts can surf for fresh meat online. Fresh meat that writes messages like, *I am looking for good woman with pure heart to be precious for all rest of my life.* Like, *I am good lover, v understanding.* Like, *I dream of London but would be happy in Norwich or other small England town.* These boys ignore the sea of tight shimmering virgins to focus on us, the second hand, every one hoping for things local girls can't provide. They're wise young owls, Hassan and his kind. They see their parents and don't want to become them. They see the glorious mountains behind this complex and know they might as well be a mirage. Three days ago, Hassan asked if he could kiss my hand and I damn near stuffed him in my beach bag.

Actually, in that moment, looking at the surrounding waiters and lifeguards, I thought about taking home a whole harem of them, a different boy for each day of the week. Does that mean I'm losing my mind, or finding it? I didn't think of such things while chatting with *FunBoy1985* at 3 a.m., glass of white wine in hand, but it occurs to me now that perhaps Hassan is on the forum too, under a different name. Maybe we're having the same conversation in two different places. In a universe with no God, or one too shy to interfere, not merciful enough to have let you survive what the judge called *the kind of senseless attack that leads one to wonder whether humanity is worth rescuing*, Hassan is right to pursue several options. My codename was *Rue de la Liberation*, the name of the road the complex is on. What names they have for things here, Jonathan! Liberation Street! Are they trying to make us laugh?

I've not told anyone about us, or what happened. You're mine only.

The other night I went swimming in the hotel pool, long after they turned off the heat. It was dark but for the occasional lamp lighting the palm trees and the hum from hotel rooms up above. I swam twenty lengths, thirty, then pressed on to fifty and beyond, till I lost count. I could feel the temperature dropping but didn't get out until I could hardly breathe. I staggered at the side of the pool, until Hassan appeared as if by magic, as if from under the pool, to steady me. He was dressed in a white short-sleeved shirt, shorts and sandals (not topless for once); he must have been on his way back to his room, or perhaps to the bus stop. (I don't know where the workers sleep. I realised then that I hadn't thought about where he lives at all.) He placed his hands on my forearms and led me to the door, then the lift by reception, then to the corridor on the nineteenth floor.

Once we were through the door into my room he insisted on putting me, still in my swimsuit, to bed like a baby. *Sshh, Christine,* said Hassan, rubbing a towel through my hair. *No troubles. Forget everything before.* Then he picked up a comb and stroked it through the strands of brown and silver, telling me a story about his childhood as I shivered, the lactic acid washing every part of me. The story Hassan told was something to do with his mother's hands. Or was I imagining that? He seemed to be in no rush. To have nowhere else to go. Either that or I was, for that moment anyway, his only care. As I began to feel myself slipping from consciousness he kissed my lips, tiptoed towards the exit and left, closing the door so softly that it hardly made any sound.

I slept without dreaming but the peace didn't last. In the morning I woke, joints throbbing, amazed to find myself alone. How could this be? How could it be happening? Again! Jonathan, I was overtaken by the urge to search under the bed to check you weren't hiding there. I lifted the pillows. Cast off the sheet. Slapped the bedside table with my hand, trying to strike away the image of you lying beside me, no longer breathing. This image was replaced in my mind by another, of Hassan in the en suite bathroom, shaving, a towel round his waist, singing loudly as if trying to prove how undeniably *alive* he was. But when I checked, no, he wasn't in my bathroom. Was he already on shift? Did he work all day and all night as well? Did he have days off? Sure only of my solitude, I stumbled over to the French windows, looked down onto the pool and watched the children splashing about in there. I can't continue like this much longer, Jonathan. Can you understand? Or would you rather I swan-dive from the veranda? Some women in my position make a sacrifice of themselves. Their funerals are steady affairs. The eulogies focus on their dedication to long-dead husbands. How these women didn't want to live without them. How that's what love is, and how it really is a beautiful thing and, despite the tragedy, we should all try to understand. I took one more look at the pool, then went inside.

An hour later I left the hotel room and headed towards the beach, texting Beata on the way. *How is your brave new world?* I asked her. *Mine not so brave.* For a woman with such a high-powered job, she always seems to have spare thumbs and time to reply. Her answer came through seconds later: *You are a predator. Grrrr. Now POUNCE!* I can't explain it, I shouldn't be expected to, but those capital letters made me feel so far away from my friend that, Jonathan, if you had risen up from the sand and explained right then and there that Beata and I were living on different planets, well, I would certainly have believed you. I turned off the phone and threw it into my handbag. I looked at my watch. Decided to put on a little make-up.

When I arrived at the beach I took out a paperback and settled down under a thatched umbrella for the afternoon, close to Hassan but not too close. It doesn't do to look desperate. I watched him at work, thinking how he smells of rich, thick Turkish coffee (strange given we're not in Turkey), and how he might look good propped up in our back garden, overlooking the pond like some kind of exotic gnome.

I took a spot between two others, both of these creatures, if you don't mind me saying so, making me look like an Oscar statuette by comparison. (At least I've made an effort. Some women have no shame.) Hassan is polite, of course, but he's not interested. Neither of those wear any rings on any of their fingers — and from the way Hassan stands, shoulders straight as a ruler, you can tell he likes a challenge. What male with an ounce of worth likes a door swinging open? Especially when that open door is a semi-retired Bed & Breakfast proprietor from Blackpool with dyed red hair, an accent like sawdust and a spare tyre the size of Marrakech? I summoned Hassan, ordered a mojito and threatened to sunbathe topless — if he behaved himself. He went to get my drink while heat raced from my lips to my toes then back up again. Yesterday was a good day.

Perhaps you'd have been proud of me, making this great not-quite-statement of what the young insist on calling *moving on,* as if love was something one picked up for a while, fingered, then dropped, leaving no after-effects. Perhaps you'd have been appalled. But how long is it appropriate to wait? Exactly how miserable are you supposed be before cracking? As Hassan served, I bundled my hair on top of my head, a chopstick through the centre and several strands of hair left to dangle, drawing his attention to that neck and shoulders he saw close-up in my hotel room, the same neck and shoulders you used to prefer me to put out on show. *Let them see what they can't touch,* you'd say, making me both a prize and a threat. As I am now. Briefly I considered kicking the mojito onto the sand. Isn't this exactly the sort of humiliation women like me spend lifetimes trying to avoid? Rather than overturning the glass, I drained it, and Hassan came soon after with a replacement. *On the house,* he said. *Please. A present. Welcome in Africa.* I protested but he said, *For most beautiful woman in all the beach.* Be fair to the boy, he's smart — he didn't specify outer or inner beauty. I accepted the drink without comment, then hardly moved for the next four hours.

The restaurant delivers food direct to the loungers, so I ordered from my seat and ate lunch horizontal, only rising every hour or so to paddle in the water or go to the Ladies. (Sometimes the same thing. One can only leave one's possessions unattended on a sun lounger so often without basically asking to be burgled.) In between conversing with Hassan, and also one or two other waiters and lifeguards attracted like flies to the only lamp in the room, I read an entire book, one given to me by a snub-nosed woman in the complex who said I looked like I needed a thrill. (How could she tell?) Anyway, this book was about a disabled woman in 19th Century Germany who overcomes her own overpowering shyness and the prejudices of the society around her to become some sort of striptease or burlesque artist in Hungary (this is supposed to be a *happy* ending?). It's possible the main character was a lesbian. I don't know why I was compelled to continue reading, but at least that's one more book in the world I don't have to look at and wonder, *would I enjoy that?* And there are worse ways I could spend my remaining days than lying under the earth's life force reading mediocre filth. I would be doing less damage than most. Beata would approve. Though she'd like me to be more proactive.

As I read and read, only half concentrating, sun-bronzed boys in shorts fussed over the line of us, as if they were born to serve. I come back to this same spot every day, pretending I'm not watching them slink up and down the sand, sniffing the widows and divorcées, weighing up the least unsavoury option — no doubt trying not to think about what services they'd have to provide, for how long, and how it might feel, several years from now, to break for real freedom once the bedroom had simply become somewhere for sleeping and both sides were ready to trade in.

I think about these things sometimes.

When I have my eyes closed and the sun is doing the work of three, I imagine Hassan's future, the girl he'll meet in a bar, ten years from now. The Gayle or Patricia or Tracy-Ann he'll fall in love with. How he'll tell his shining young thing that although some find it difficult to understand, though some laugh, he really is grateful to the woman who liberated him from his past, the home that was really no home at all, and how without her he wouldn't now be the proud owner of a British passport, a chain of coffee shops and a 1969 Cadillac, the car his devout father always secretly wanted but was never able to buy. As Hassan will tell Patricia, at this point in the future, his father will be receiving letters every week, posted lovingly (along with generous contributions to the family finances) to the humble village shack less than fifty miles from this complex where I now lie, topping up my tan. *Papa,* the letters will say, *I made a life here.* They'll say, *Here are pictures of your grandchildren. And yes, I know Christine was rude to you but please, understand that without her I'd still be serving mojitos. Also, she taught me everything a good lover needs to know.* Hassan will be relating all this to Patricia. She'll clamp her hands round his cheeks, draw him close, wipe a tear away and whisper, *I get it, baby. Now shut up and show me what you learned.*

Every minute I spend thinking about this bullshit is a minute I don't spend missing you, which makes it time well spent: what are my other options? Reading about the voracious sexual appetites of German prostitutes, ordering cocktails from the local eye candy and trying not to bawl like a child. I won't let that happen, Jonathan. If I cry, even once, I won't survive it. Some things one feels one knows.

I look around this country you wanted to come to, and I'm frozen into wonder. You only said it once, a light comment in the middle of dinner three nights before you were murdered in our bed — *you know where I'd like to see?* — and maybe it was a fleeting interest. Maybe it was something you hardly even meant, or you meant somewhere different and got mixed up. Maybe you'd secretly wanted to visit here, researched the place for years in travel books and fallen in love with photographs, maybe you'd bought flights for our anniversary and never got the chance to tell me. That's death. You don't get to ask questions. You're left with a vague sense of the unknowable and a daughter guessing blindly at *what Daddy would have wanted*. I can't know what you wanted. I can only guess. So here I am, representing us both on this beach, wondering whether to jump into a new life. If you delay, others swoop. I'm not the only passport here.

This morning I woke to an email on my phone: Beata writing from some conference in Krakow where she's giving a paper on climate change. She's taken Youssef with her; they plan to see a few sights. She wants to see the Jewish Quarter (by which she means she wants to test-drive the bars in the Jewish Quarter). She wants to show Youssef the Da Vinci in a museum with a name I can't pronounce. Beata's message is all short sentences and exclamation marks. Questions and answers. She says revolution is coming to this place, she's heard talk in the corridors. *Do you know?* she asks. *Are you safe? It's racing up the coast,* she says. *They want democracy.* Well, they might soon have it, who knows? They'd hardly report such things here. But it'll take more than a revolution to bring change to the resort, and by the time it arrives Hassan will have missed his chance. Democracy is all very well but the poor usually remain poor whoever is in charge. No wonder they fawn on the beaches.

Now I stand on my veranda once more, scrolling up and down Beata's message, rereading, not really reading at all, wondering if I should head down to the beach and thinking that really, now is the time. I sit down in the room, fan pushing cold air into the heat, and I start writing to Amanda, fingers clumsy on the touchscreen. *My darling girl,* my message begins. For a moment I think she'll understand. But I only get halfway through the first sentence — *I have met* — before Amanda's imagined reply stops me. I imagine her suggesting I come home, imagine her instructing me to *do so alone*. But I can't promise that, or anything. There's no telling what prisoners might do given a penknife and half a chance. I delete the message, consider starting another one, inviting her out here to join me, then I put the phone down and apply sun cream instead. Shoulders, arms, neck. Legs, face, feet. I sit up. I look around, twirling the loose ring on my wedding finger. Hassan is on the beach, surrounded by vultures.

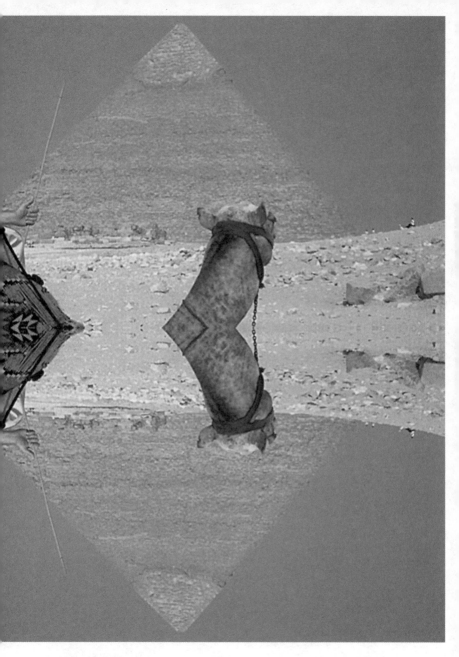

Alles wat ek verwag het om te gee vir my vreugde en wat [...] my oorreed om die reis te onderneem het my teleurgesteld, maar uit dat baie teleurstelling, ek het 'n onverwagte onderwys verkry.

ORIENTATION #3

What we now call the Amazon rainforest has been in existence, in one way or another, for 55 million years. It probably formed in the Eocene Epoch[11], and over that time the make-up of Earth's most mysterious landscape has formed and reformed more times than most human minds can comprehend. Change is ongoing, but the last 21,000 years have seen significant shifts in vegetation and climate. Scientists estimate that humankind began settling in the Amazon basin 11,000 years ago — then trouble came to town. 2005 saw the worst drought on record, and in 2008, a World Wildlife Fund report said half the rainforest will be lost by 2030. Livestock ranching, wildfire, agriculture

---

[11] The Eocene Epoch lasted from approximately 56 million to 34 million years ago. It is a major division of the geologic timescale and the second of the Paleogene Period in the Cenozoic Era. The Eocene runs from the end of the Palaeocene Epoch to the beginning of the Oligocene Epoch.

and logging are murdering this place, and wasting no time about it. So if visitors are thinking about postponing their trip, I don't recommend it. Book your tickets and get moving. Swim here if you have to. Soon, there won't be much left to see.

Visitors to this secluded corner of the rainforest will be brought in as part of a small group, accompanied by a guide dressed like an Aussie surfer who's so laid back that sometimes it'll seem like he's just a knowledgeable tourist. Leonardo is a short, stocky man in his late twenties employed to take visitors trekking, fishing and swimming over the next few days, with the standard Eco Package Monday to Friday deal which is popular with the steady stream of Amazon virgins coming through. Every week Leonardo does the pick-up from the Eco Centre in one of the northern districts of Manaus. He'll welcome you like an old friend, help you load bags into the back of the van, then weave slowly through the roads to the water. You hope you're nearly there but he laughs and says, *Now, we start!*

Some visitors will be so intoxicated by the humidity, the smells and energy of Manaus that they might not recognise it as a city at all, but something more like hell. The heat is punishing. The traffic is wild, the markets chaotic and many westerners will wish they'd never arrived here. Even Leonardo isn't keen; he's from Salvador and prefers the life there. *More colour, less busy, cooler music,* he says. But Manaus has two million inhabitants and most people here haven't heard of where you're from either. If they visited Cardiff or Newcastle, they probably wouldn't see the positives. So Leonardo says be respectful and watch those digital cameras. *It might be a pain in the ass to you, but it's life and death to the shit-kickers of Manaus.* Leonardo learned English from MTV and sounds like he's from California.

Which goes to show that either he's a pretty clever guy, or they watch too much American TV out here. He explains, in his silky West Coast accent, that you'll be making your own food. This isn't a hotel.

Manaus makes for an appropriate starter, as the Amazon rainforest is the only place many visitors will have ever been on planet Earth that, to them, doesn't look like Earth at all. The Eco Camp you're staying in is deep in the jungle and you have to pass through several worlds to get there. First, a one hour boat ride out of the city, then a one hour ride in a jeep over treacherous, uneven land where there are no roads, only patches of grass and stone, then another hour or two in a canoe. This canoe has been waiting for you at the water's edge, beside a hut where Gabriel the old goatherd hacks apart then sells watermelons. What he does with the money, nobody knows. You can't spend any within a fifty mile radius and he never leaves. Meanwhile, Leonardo will chat through each stage of the journey — snakes the size of your whole body, insects that can kill in an instant. All the joys and horrors of Amazonas. Then he asks with a grin, *Have you seen the movie Arachnaphobia?* The way he smiles and puffs his chest out, he's definitely flirting with you. It's hard to be sure, the atmosphere is melting your senses, but maybe he's flirting with your husband as well. Either that or preparing to fight. Already, anything seems possible.

In the rainforest, you'll be amongst wonders you never even knew existed — birds that look like monkeys, fish that look like crocodiles. According to the National Geographic, these tropical forests in the heart of the Amazon basin *are some of the most biodiverse areas on Earth and home to many species found nowhere else*. So don't daydream: there's no shame in taking photos. Even if you'd dressed as the locals do, it'd be obvious you're a tourist, and besides, the animals won't sue. Some of them pose, and what poses they pull! Even visitors who've never had time for religion may ask themselves, *who is responsible for making all this? And how should I go about thanking them?* More people find God in the Amazon than in Texas prisons. And life expectancy is longer here too.

Visitors will notice that most trees are three-quarters submerged in water and crawling with the wildest of wildlife. The liquid below will be thick and bubbling hot, a meaty soup full up with piranhas, fireflies and three thousand species of fish, including the world's most diverse variety of electric fish — also many other things you don't want to think about too much because you're pretty squeamish. Tonight you'll be canoeing into the Eco Camp at dusk, a time when the trees look like shadows and the shadows look like monsters, so keep a hold of your mind and don't let go. On arrival, Leonardo will show you to the wooden hut on stilts you'll be calling home, and without your husband noticing he'll pat you lightly on the bottom. *Chill out!* he'll say. *Have fun! But don't rock this baby too much, yeah? Foundations are weak. And under here — SNAP! — crocodiles.* Then he'll wink at you both before leaving.

So this is your first night in the Amazon. You've wanted to come for twenty years and now, here you are. Dad was wrong! You're not all talk! Haul up the blinds as the sun begins to dip and notice how, though the sky is blue on the left and right of your vision, there's a bright red shock in the middle, a Jackson Pollock splurge that makes it seem like wildfire is dotted through the air. Think to yourself, *This is my sky too.* Take a head torch and keep an eye on the water at dusk; with luck, you'll spot wild pink dolphins only yards from your bed. At first, these animals look like they've been skinned, like their inner body muscle is on show, but there's no need to hide. Sit out on the jetty, dangle your feet off the side and watch them dance. Have you ever felt so alive? Or small? In the black of night see how bright stars can be, and wonder why they aren't so bright in Swindon.

Tuesday morning, Leonardo takes you bird spotting. He won't let either of you help row the boat. It's a pride thing and he's the only one who knows how to get back to the camp, so visitors will just have to let it go. Marvel at what he points out as you pass — scarlet macaws, harpy eagles, ospreys, red-bill toucans — and that's just what he can see. According to Leonardo, many of the birds here are tourists too, passing through on their way from the north or south of Brazil, checking out the scenery and scouting for lunch. He also says some Amazonian birds take a partner for life. When one partner dies, the other commits suicide, jumping off the tree's highest branch like it's the Sydney Harbour Bridge and there's no point going on. He says to you, *This is true love, no?* Your husband grips your hand and tells Leonardo, *Yeah, love is a real killer.*

As you'll see for the rest of your trip, the rainforest rewards visitors with astounding beauty but it does make them sweat for it. Your shirt is always damp here, your legs keep sticking together. Your body can't get enough air and always feels like it's gasping. Meanwhile, the local children leap playfully from land to water, water to land, laughing and running, glistening and taut as if their bodies contain all the energy they'll ever need. For them, the temperature's just right. Though this is your planet too you can't agree, and, even when you're aware of feeling at home here, you wonder if you can cope with the heat, even for another hour. It's been obvious since the first night: air conditioning is a serious business for tourists. At 2 am the generator goes off and the temperature rockets.

Meanwhile, your cabin wobbles when the wind is high. Visitors will notice how, even as they wash the wet film off their arms, it resurfaces again instantly. You'll always be hot here, but who cares? When you're showering outside the hut, a skinny local boy called Pedro canoes past and waves. You wave back, forgetting you're naked. Then you remember, and laugh out loud. It's addictive.

There's much to do during the rest of the trip — before visitors leave on Friday they'll drink the milk out of a tree. On Thursday night they'll catch a fish with a piece of string and grill it for supper while the crickets chirp, loud as bombs. Between then and now you'll share precious moments with your husband, the most precious you'll ever have together, and when you make love in the blistering, sticky-slick heat, the climax will feel like a surprise so strong and welcome that you'll want to black out. Before here, you thought such things were a Hollywood rumour, designed to keep people forever searching, but on Thursday night you'll cry with love. In the total darkness unique to this place it'll feel like your husband is crawling over you, planting kisses as he goes, a wet, poisonous insect who chooses not to bite, at least not yet. He'll hold you and not ask any questions when you tell him you've changed your mind — you do want children after all. He understands. This place, it does things. And sometimes it's best just to accept.

On Friday, a few hours before leaving, you'll visit an Amazonian family in their huts — this will be the only time you feel you're exploiting the locals. But Leonardo insists it's the best way to show respect, and anyway, it's your own fault. You told Leonardo you play guitar, so the children of the family take the out-of-tune classical instrument off the straw hut wall and make you play a song. These tiny people, their pupils are huge and they wait for you. When you protest you don't know what to play, a six year old girl will shout, *BEATLES!* as if she's been taught to do so. You don't understand why The Beatles are popular everywhere on earth but so what? You're supposed to be joining in. You play her *Hey Jude*, getting all the chords wrong, forgetting the words to the verses and accidentally having a good time. The children give you a gift. It looks like a thick leaf but break it open and there's fruit inside. Apparently, the Eco Camp looks after them so there's no need to buy; you get a necklace anyway and wear the delicate thing till it falls apart.

In years to come, you'll forget these adventures. In the end, even the girl and the Beatles will be gone from your mind, the outside shower and pink dolphins too. Why this is, you don't know. As you've realised these past few days, there's a lot you don't know. But today's the Wednesday of the trip, and it's the one day you'll remember for the rest of your life. Wake up early, go walking with Leonardo and the rest of the group for a couple of hours in the jungle, while Leonardo explains how much has been wiped out here. The history lesson is exhausting and it sounds like when he's blaming the white man, he wants you to say sorry. Maybe you should, but put it at the back of your mind until later. Now, get your boots on — or more likely, your sandals. We're going to have some fun.

Locals arrive for the weekly match as they travel everywhere: by canoe. Ground which is steady underfoot is rare here but the football enthusiasts of the Amazon have found an area large enough to play. They've imported two full size goals from Manaus to a place which can only be found by the most skilled boatmen, young men who glide between the trees of the Amazon as if they were born knowing the routes. It's a gorgeous spot and the pitch isn't too rough. It hurts to play barefoot but everyone else is doing it so why not? You want your soles to be like the rest of these boys, like leather. Some of them won't tackle you at all but that only means you'll see more of the ball, and at least they let you play. Be careful though — if you shoot too hard and the ball goes in the water, someone will have to dive in and get it for you. Which makes André the goalkeeper grumpy.

Throughout the game, new players and spectators keep arriving on the shore, adding to the carnival. Players' mothers, sisters, grandparents too, tumble out of canoes and take their seats on the sidelines. Sometimes they sing.

Any late arrivals will immediately notice the tourists are losing. It's the same every day. The teams may be different but the Away team, made up of whoever's coming through to the Eco Camp that week (and this week that's you), can't cope with the forty-degree-plus heat which beats down here for most of the day. The locals know nothing else. Their ball skills remain undiminished. Pedro, who owns the ball, knows the weaknesses of the tourists and schedules matches for noon. Only Leonardo, who told you he was a professional, a cult hero in the German 3rd Division, struggles to keep up with the pace. The locals are lean. Leonardo asks to be substituted. He's probably lying about Germany. But too much tour-guiding and falling for European women, who always go home and never return, has turned Leonardo into a tortoise. Forget him. Enjoy yourself. Some of these boys joke with the tourists but even Pedro will agree, this day is a present from the Amazon you can always keep.

Mostly you've spent the last twenty minutes staggering about the pitch, panting. Your husband too. (He's now taking a break, refuelling with water.) Surely, you both think, some of these guys could make the national team. They do keepy-uppies for fun, they play tiki-taka like

Barcelona, calling each other *Messi* and *Iniesta*. They score nine goals while the tourists score none. And then the ball trickles towards you, you run towards the water, and kick, just as your whole body seems to be pulled away. Then you're on the floor, looking up at the Jackson Pollock sky and wondering if this is still your life. The call goes up, *Whoa!* Locals crowd round to check you're okay. They want you to sit. One points to his canoe, offering to take you home (or to a doctor?) and the player who brought you down is sent, shame-faced, from the pitch. It's a penalty, and you insist on staying to take it. Some things you have to do. It doesn't matter if you score. Also, André is twelve years old, so you fancy your chances. You look around at the people you've met this week — the ones now clapping and stamping their feet in anticipation — and wish you were born here. Then you place the ball on the spot and concentrate.

Your husband is smiling, cheering you on. Tonight he'll kiss where you hit your head and christen it your *Amazon bump*. Right now, he believes you're going to score.

That time I took a penalty in the Amazon. In many future moments, this will be a pure memory. Briefly you'll forget the horrors of your husband's illness and his slow death, that his brother hasn't even called once since his funeral to see how you're coping. It won't matter that you somehow chose the wrong career or could never bring yourself to tell anyone about that miscarriage. Whatever mistakes you make and the ways you make them, this will always be yours. As the years pass, the story will inflate. The foul will become more vicious, the penalty more dramatic, the Brazilian players seven or eight foot tall. Even the setting will amplify, the audience swelling to hundreds while the temperature in the Amazon soars to boiling. None of it matters.

This will remind you of a time when you were free, and you'll be glad you didn't stay at home.

Credits &
Acknowledgements

I have been working towards this collection since 2009. Whenever I was asked to write a short story for a book, magazine or project, I tried to do it in a way that would later fit into a series of travel stories. Once I had a few of these I began to write them independently, expanding the book into what it is now. I am grateful to the original publishers of these stories, who have generously allowed me to reclaim the work here. All the stories listed below have been re-edited.

A Weekend of Freedom first appeared in *Gutter* magazine, Issue #2, published by Freight Books in August 2010.

Do All Things With Love was first published in the *Edinburgh Review*, Issue #132, in September 2011.

After Drink You Can Turn Earth Upside Down was commissioned by the Edinburgh International Book Festival and first appeared as part of the *Elsewhere* collection, a four book series published by Cargo/McSweeney's in August 2012. This was part of the book *There*. It was also published in *Rampike* magazine in Canada.

Intervention was published in the Unbound Press annual anthology in November 2012. It was translated into Serbian by Ljupka Jovanovic and appeared in *Književni Magazin* in Winter 2012.

I Know My Team and I Shall Not Be Moved was published in *Roads Ahead*, a short story anthology published by Tindal Street Press in October 2009.

Orientation #2 was translated into Serbian by Ljupka Jovanovic and appeared in *Književni Magazin* in Winter 2012.

The Hips on Planet Latina first appeared in *Gutter* magazine, Issue #4, published by Freight Books in August 2011, under the title **Why Nothing Works No. 2.**

We're All Gonna Have the Blues was commissioned for *Beacons: Stories for Our Not-So-Distant Future*, an anthology published by Oneworld Publications in April 2013.

59 Places to Fuck in Arizona was first published in *Irish Pages*, Volume 6, Number 2, in January 2012.

Liberation Street was published in *Gutter* magazine, Issue #8, in February 2013.

'I Want to Be a Tourist' by Kapka Kassabova was published in *Geography for the Lost*, (Bloodaxe Books, 2007) and is used with permission from the author and Bloodaxe Books.

The title and concept for **The Monogamy Optician** came from a poem by Caroline Bird of the same name, from her collection *Watering Can* (Carcanet, 2009) and is used with permission from the author. Several lines from the poem are also used, with the kind permission of Carcanet Press.

Orientation #1 was written with the essential assistance of the Danish poet Carsten René Nielsen, so thank you, Carsten. The story quotes from Daniele Pantano's poem 'The Axiology of Taste' from his collection *The Oldest Hands in the World* (Black Lawrence Press, 2010), and Daniele's words are stolen with permission from the author.

Kaikkea sitä odotin antamaan minulle iloksi ja jotka [...] suostutteli minua tekemään matkaa oli minulle pettymys — mutta ulos juuri pettymyksen, olen hankkinut odottamaton koulutusta.

Several of these stories were written or revised while I was Writer-in-Residence in Tršic, Serbia, in August 2012. I am grateful to Vuk, to the Ministry of Culture, and to everyone who made me feel so welcome. (Sorry, my Serbian story didn't make the cut — but it may appear elsewhere one day.) Meanwhile, my thanks go to Adrian at Freight for his unwavering faith, Anneliese for the edit, the advice and the track listing, and to my dedicated agent, Jenny Brown. Thanks go to the friends I made on my travels, the friends at home who held me together when there was adversity to triumph over, also to those writers who influenced this collection through their words, written or spoken.

And thank you, Caroline.

"Everything that I expected to give me delight and which [...] persuaded me to undertake the journey had disappointed me — but out of that very disappointment, I have acquired an unexpected education."

André Gide, author of *Voyage au Congo* and *Le Retour de Tchad*

Segala sesuatu yang saya harapkan untuk memberikan kesenangan dan yang [...] membujuk saya untuk melakukan perjalanan telah kecewa saya -. Tapi dari kekecewaan yang sangat, saya telah memperoleh pendidikan yang tak terduga.

FREIGHT
BOOKS

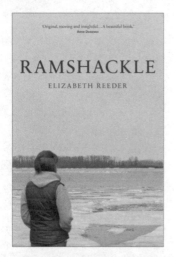

Ramshackle

Elizabeth Reeder

RRP   **£8.99**
ISBN   **978-0956613-57-8**

Shortlisted for the Scottish First Book of the Year, this is a beautiful and haunting debut about abandonment and self-discovery in the spirit of Daniel Woodrell's *Winter's Bone*.

"Ramshackle deserves a place in the bestseller charts: a novel that deals with the primal fear of abandonment and portrays it through a vividly realised 15 year-old girl we can't help but identify with."
The Herald

FREIGHT BOOKS

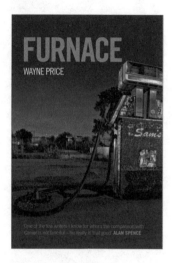

Furnace

Wayne Price

RRP **£8.99**

ISBN **978-0956613-58-5**

Long-listed for the Frank O'Connor International Short Story Award and Shortlisted for the Scottish First Book of the Year 2012. Wayne Price combines the fearlessness of Raymond Carver and subtlety of William Trevor with the unflinching vision of Paul Bowles.

"This debut collection of short stories is being hailed as the emergence of a new talent, a claim I'm tempted to take seriously"
The Herald

FREIGHT
BOOKS

The Falling Sky

Pippa Goldschmidt

RRP **£8.99**
ISBN **978-1-908754-14-1**

Jeanette is a young, solitary post-doctoral researcher who has dedicated her life to studying astronomy. Struggling to compete in a prestigious university department dominated by egos and incompetents, and caught in a cycle of brief and unsatisfying affairs, she travels to a mountain-top observatory in Chile to focus on her research. There Jeanette stumbles upon evidence that will challenge the fundamentals of the universe, drawing her into conflict with her colleagues and the scientific establishment, but also casting her back to the tragic loss that defined her childhood.

FREIGHT
BOOKS

The Hairdresser of Harare
Tendai Huchu

RRP **£8.99**

ISBN **978-0956613-58-5**

Vimbai is the star hairdresser of her salon, the smartest in Harare, Zimbabwe, until the enigmatic Dumisani appears. Losing many of her best customers to this good-looking, smooth-talking young man, Vimbai fears for her job, vital if she's to provide for her young child. But in a remarkable reversal the two becomes allies. Soon they are running their own Harare salon, attracting the wealthiest and most powerful clients in the city. But disaster is near, as Vimbai soon uncovers Dumi's secret, a discovery that will result in brutality and tragedy, testing their relationship to the very limit.

FREIGHT
BOOKS

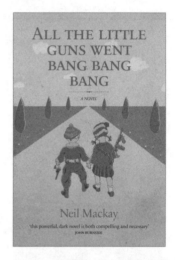

All the Little Guns Went Bang Bang Bang

Neil Mackay

RRP   **£8.99**

ISBN   **978-1-908754-28-8**

Pearse Furlong and May-Belle Mulholland are two normal eleven year-olds meeting one summer in small town Antrim, Northern Ireland, in the early 1980s. They have little in common except a shared experience of violent, abusive parents. They form an unlikely alliance and as their games and shared fantasies spin out of control their friendship becomes something much darker, with theft, arson, sickening brutality — and eventually murder — all lying ahead.